ANDR

Rob was the last defender left alive. He said, "You're a cyborg, just like Steele. That's why you're so strong!"

"I'm not like Steele, sweetheart. I'm *better*," Miseri said.

He charged the lady terminator. He was a good soldier, but he was only human. She plucked the knife from his hands and bent it almost double with a flick of her slim wrists.

Then she grabbed his head in both hands and broke his neck.

MOLTEN STEELE

The Steele Series From The Berkley Publishing Group

MOLTEN STEELE

S. L. HUNTER

BERKLEY BOOKS, NEW YORK

MOLTEN STEELE

A Berkley Book / published by arrangement with
the author

PRINTING HISTORY
Berkley edition / October 1991

ISBN: 0-425-12965-9

A BERKLEY BOOK ® TM 757,375
Berkley Books are published by The Berkley Publishing Group,
200 Madison Avenue, New York, New York 10016.
The name "Berkley" and the "B" logo
are trademarks belonging to Berkley Publishing Corporation.

PRINTED IN THE UNITED STATES OF AMERICA

10 9 8 7 6 5 4 3 2 1

For Melodie,
for being generally swell

PART ONE

COLD BLOOD

Prologue _____

"Hold it!" Zane whispered urgently to his partner, Hodge. He stopped. The stubby, caseless assault rifle in his hands began to quiver as if it had a life of its own. "I heard something . . . didn't you hear it?"

His partner looked at him through the darkness. The late-spring night was pleasantly cool, even after you'd been out in it an hour or so. The moon had hours ago slipped down into the volcanic haze that lined the western horizon. The sky above was clear, and the feeble light of the stars turned the mountains that seemed to hang above them to the east and the desert sliding away beyond the wire west to the river valley to ghostly shapes and shadow masses. A few kilometers to the north, the Christ of the Sandias, one hundred and twenty-five feet tall, cast His gentle radiance into the night: red, green, yellow, white.

"It's the wind," Hodge said in a normal voice. He was short-er, heavier, and older than the rangy, beak-nosed Zane, and the hair the never-ending wind ruffled on his bare head was thin-ner. He carried a full-auto shotgun, bullpup-pattern, its thick magazine mounted behind the pistol grip. The piece was cur-rently slung over his back.

"I tell you I _heard_ something!" Zane insisted. Starlight glit-tered on the curve of wide-open eyeballs. "It was a thump of some kind, like somebody jumped over the wire."

3

Hodge's wide lipless mouth twisted in disgust. He jerked a thumb at the wire. "We got a three-meter fence with knife-wire coils up top, 'case you hadn't noticed till now. Nobody's comin' over that, you dumb-ass—"

Behind him a shadow-flicker, black on blackness. Zane opened his mouth to warn him. Hodge saw, started to turn his head.

Black fingers came around Hodge's head, gripped his chin from behind. They pulled. Hodge's head turned right around with a sound like a 10mm handgun.

Hodge dropped straight to the *caliche* hardpan, his body flopping big belly down, hands fluttering like birds. Zane looked down in horror. Hodge was staring right up at him from between his own shoulders with dead eyes.

Something stood behind Hodge's twitching corpse. Forgetting the hand-talker at his belt, Zane opened his mouth to scream.

Hardness hit him in the solar plexus. The air blasted out of him in a voiceless rush.

The southeastern section of Albuquerque was represented in the City Council by Barbara Brand. What that really meant was that Brand ran the district like a personal fief, constantly seeking what advantage she could find over her four rival council members, and all the while pretending that she and they ruled the disaster-shattered city as its legitimate government. Things had changed in the Río Grande Valley since the volcanoes had erupted two years before . . .

Brand's inner sanctum and stronghold was the proprietary vest-pocket suburb of Four Hills, nestled against the hip of the Manzano Mountains. She and her inner circle lived in big fortified houses around the former country club, with its broad artificial pond and the former golf course she had converted to a park, which boasted a somewhat scraggly botanical garden, a stable for her Arabian horses, and a pasture for her flock of pet sheep.

The tiny development stuck like an aneurysm into the military reservation surrounding Kirtland Air Force Base. Out this way, a few klicks beyond runway's end, the base was desert indistinguishable from the rest of the empty land stretching south toward Los Lunas and west toward LA. Only a few random dirt roads led up to the perimeter out of the waste.

Still, there was no love lost between the various council members and the base officers, who clung to the notion that they were the legitimate representatives of a Federal authority which had been decaying steadily for years, and shriveled away to nothing with the first crack of Eruption. Kirtland's commander, Major General Paul Whiteman, was a reconciliatory kind of man; his second in command, Colonel George Donelson, commanding officer of the 223rd Special Security Group was a harder case, not to mention more ambitious. But like the other power players between the ramparts of the Sandia and Manzano mountain ranges and the recently revived volcanoes west of the river, Kirtland was not exactly overloaded with resources.

To date they had never mustered any moves more aggressive than the occasional light probe, easily deniable—hot pursuit of fugitives, say, or a few rowdies getting likkered up of a Saturday night and lofting a few M-91 rockets over the wire for shits'n'grins. *Sorry, Councilor Brand, but, y'know, boys will be boys.* All the same, Brand's security kept a wary eye on the perimeter, with patrols and guardposts armed with antitank missiles more than competent to bust open the armored cars which were the heaviest hardware Kirtland—with most of what planes the progressive disintegration of the once-United States had left it disabled by Eruption and kept on the ground by lack of replacement parts—could throw.

Delbert threw down his Albuquerque *Journal/Tribune* crossword puzzle with a grunt of disgust. "What you drinking there, Sarge?"

Sergeant Nguyen was graveyard shift commander for the security detachment stationed in the boarded-up former convenience store at the southwest corner of the Four Hills perimeter. "Tea," he said simply. He was a trim man of medium height, with a precise moustache and heavy-lidded eyes. He didn't talk much.

Grunting, Delbert heaved his bulk out of his lawn chair. "Lemme have a slug."

The sergeant held up the red plaid thermos jug. Delbert swaggered up to him, accepted it, took a hit right from the wide mouth.

He coughed, spewed liquid all over the squad room, drawing outraged cries from his buddies.

"Holy Christ, Delbert!" yelped Hagar, who wore his white-blond surfer-boy hair longer than Nguyen particularly cared for. "What's gotten into you?"

"I'm poisoned. What is this stuff?"

"Tea, as I told you," Nguyen said.

"It tastes like cat piss."

"It is a non-caffeinated herbal tea."

"That explains it. You got me drinking *boiled weeds*."

"'Infusion' was what we called that, back in high school biology," said Norris, skinny, black, and something of a geek, who sat beside the card table that held their commo set.

"Thanks for sharing that with us, Norris," Delbert said. "Whyn't you drink something with a *kick* in it there, Sarge?"

"Stimulants and narcotics are alike forbidden us by law," Nguyen said primly.

"Aw, Christ. I keep forgetting you gate-guard boys always have your eye on the rule books. It's 'cause you never get any action to occupy your minds."

"If you are aware of conduct contrary to regulations among the external security forces," Nguyen purred, "it is of course your duty to report such acts to your superiors."

"Never mind," Delbert said. "I forgot."

Del Pino knotted the fingers of his big hands together, cracked his knuckles. "We don't just sit on our asses out here, *gringo*. Colonel Donelson, he tries something every once in a while, just to see if we on our toes."

"Whoa," Norris said under his breath, catching sight of the digital clock on the wall beneath the calendar. This month the calendar photo was kittens in a basket of yarn. Councilor Brand ordered the calendars by the job-lot for her security forces. They couldn't tell her how much they appreciated them.

Norris' long spider-leg fingers punched buttons on the console, and he murmured for the benefit of the little insect-leg mike curved in front of his mouth. With his Tony Lama boots propped on the commo table beside Norris' set, Hagar eyed Delbert critically.

"What're you bitching about, old man? Thought you'd transferred over here to get away from all the excitement."

"I applied because I'm getting too old to play hide-and-seek in the rubble with Great Satan bikers and Maynet and DiStefano's merry elves. But I can tell you, son, I *wish* I'd gotten switched over before that fuckup Downtown last week."

"Hey, that was some fight, huh?" del Pino asked, leaning forward eagerly in his chair.

"Massacre was more like it, boy. We were all dug in and ready for him—us right alongside detachments from all the other council districts *and* the Crips. Same people been trying to kill us the last couple years. And I wanna tell you, the only reason that sonovabitch Steele didn't kick more of our asses was he come in a side way, got in and out before we really had a chance to respond."

Del Pino didn't bother to conceal his contempt. "How tough could he be? He's just one man."

"He's a cyborg, junior. Cyber-fucking-netic organism. Except there weren't too much organic to him. He's just a big old nysteel skeleton, and the bullets bounce right off."

"Sergeant Nguyen," Norris said, "Hodge and Zane missed their call-in, and I can't raise them on the phone."

"They're probably going down on each other in some arroyo," del Pino said.

"Let their stupid batteries run down, more like," Hagar said.

"Hagar, you and Sampson go out and find them," Nguyen said. "You may take the vehicle."

"Wow, Sarge," Hagar said. "Now we're livin' in style. Make sure you don't spoil us here." The outpost had a little Brazilian four-wheel-drive vehicle assigned to it, but the conservation-conscious Brand restricted motor vehicle use to emergencies. Patrols at night were generally conducted on foot, and in the daytime on mountain bikes.

Hagar stood up. Nguyen handed him a key on a big silver ring, and he unlocked the metal strongbox where their small arms were held. Aside from Nguyen's Ruger service sidearm on his Sam Browne belt and the longarms carried by the perimeter patrol, all weapons were kept under lock and key.

Delbert kicked Sampson's foot off the knee he had it crossed over. "Hey there, big boy. Come back to the world. You got a job to do."

Sampson lowered the magazine he was reading and pulled the headphones off his ears. Sampson had a passion for weight lifting. His enormous pectoral muscles bunched and flowed beneath his white tee-shirt, and his big black arms fairly exploded out the stub sleeves.

"That stuff'll rot your mind," Delbert said, nodding to the magazine. It was called *Muddy Wheel: Journal of New Age and Avant-Garde Ceramic Art.*

"I had a gallery show in Santa Fe," Sampson said, getting to his feet.

"Yeah, and see what happened? Valle Grande blew its stack, and now Santa Fe ain't *there* no more," Delbert said.

Hagar handed a bullpup M-27 assault rifle to Sampson, took a semiauto riot shotgun for himself. Leaving the top to the small-arms strongbox open, he headed out the front door. Sampson paused, racking the bolt on his weapon to make sure a caseless 4.7mm round was chambered.

The door had barely closed behind Hagar when it opened again. Hagar reeled inside, one step, two. He went to his knees.

Norris screamed. The right temple of Hagar's head had a nasty concave look, and the whole right side of his face was a bloody creep-show mask. He fell heavily to the floor.

The door exploded open. Nguyen's Ruger appeared as if by magic in his hard brown hand, and Delbert fumbled another M-27 out of the open strong box.

It was Zane from the perimeter patrol. He flew forward several steps, knocked over the coffee table with the chess set and hotplate on it, and sat down heavily with his legs in a spreading pool of Nguyen's nasty tea. His wrists were fastened behind his back with nylon restraints.

A woman stepped into the squad room. She was perhaps five feet eight inches tall, slim as a wand. She had on black nonreflective paint and a web utility belt. Aside from that she was stark naked.

"Don't worry about him," she said, nodding to Zane. Her voice was steady, matter-of-fact. "I didn't hurt him. I want him to be my witness."

Norris located his voice first. "T-to what?"

She laughed. It was a sound like pre-1965 silver dimes ringing on a counter. "To my killing you, of course."

Nguyen's pistol roared. The glass in the front door blew out. The woman was no longer between the pistol and the door. She was pitching forward in a blurred roll.

She uncoiled, sweeping Delbert's legs sideways out from under him with her slim, strong legs. He fell like a pole-axed steer. Nguyen was on his feet, holding his sidearm on the naked woman in a textbook two-hand Weaver stance. He fired twice. She rolled sideways out of the way as the shots knocked divots out of the thin puke-colored carpet, then jumped lithely to her feet.

Del Pino came out of his chair, lunged for her; she evaded his rush like smoke. Sampson was dancing from one foot to the other, holding his assault rifle with its barrel toward the ceiling and yelling, "Get out of the *way*, man, I can't get no shot!"

Frowning slightly with concentration, Nguyen tried to track the intruder, sliding his feet like a *karateka*, moving his whole body to bring his piece to bear. The naked woman spun. Her bare heel knocked the pistol from his hand in a scything back-kick.

She stepped forward into him, firing a straight right-hand punch as she did. Her fist sank into his sternum almost to the wrist, with a sound like a sledgehammer hitting a wood post. His eyes bulged, and blood started from the corner of his mouth, and he collapsed.

Del Pino's muscular arms came around like a hoop, pinning her arms from behind. She smiled, ground her bare muscular ass against his crotch. He gasped. She slammed the back of her head into his nose, breaking it with an audible crack. His bear-hug slackened. She snapped her arms forward, freeing them, then jerked stiffened thumbs back over her shoulders.

Del Pino shrieked like a jungle cat as her thumbs plunged into his eyes. Blood and aqueous humor spurted over her shoulders.

Vomit slopped over Sampson's big underlip. "Shit! Holy shit!" he screamed, spurting gobbets of puke from his mouth. His finger tightened convulsively on the trigger.

"*Noooo!*" Delbert howled, holding his own weapon out in front of him as a shield. It didn't do much good. A line of small red holes marched left to right across the front of his broad chest. Behind him, splintery holes appeared in the wood that covered the floor-to-ceiling front windows as Sampson slashed his flame-sputtering weapon across the space where the intruder had stood. The last rounds in the box cut del Pino's shrieks of agony short.

Sampson was still mashing the trigger back into the handgrip of the now-silent weapon when the woman came rolling across the floor at him. Before he could respond, she drove a straight kick into his nuts. He doubled, collapsed.

She rolled out from under him, popped to her feet, gymnast-light. Norris the techie sat frozen by his console, his long skinny kid face gray with fear. She grabbed him by the front of his fatigue blouse and hauled him to his feet.

"No, wait, leave me alone, I swear I won't hurt you—" he gobbled.

She caught him in a two-arm embrace, crushed him against her, stopped his babbling by driving her tongue down his throat. He writhed against her, eyes rolling like the eyes of a horse running back into a barn fire. He could feel her nipples erect against his chest, through his fatigues and the Virus-7 rap group tee-shirt beneath. His dick got hard.

She broke his spine beneath the shoulderblades and dropped him flopping.

A scuffle of feet on carpet. She spun, whipping up a circular forearm block in time to deflect a massive black fist and send it rushing harmlessly past her ear. Sampson stood, mighty chest heaving, eyes red, hunched in a boxer's stance.

Hands held up before her in mantis stance, she circled, bare feet avoiding fallen bodies and other debris as if by radar. Her small nipples were erect, standing out from aureoles that were a darker black against her black-painted breasts.

She smiled sweetly. Sampson launched a jab at her smile. She moved her head what seemed just millimeters to her left and the blow went by.

He threw a right. She dodged that too, barely seeming to move.

She twitched her own right hand. His massive left forearm moved to block. He was surprisingly fast.

Her move had been a feint, stopped before truly launched. When he blocked, her hand darted inside like a cobra striking and laid an open-palm slap on his left ear. Blood streamed.

He bellowed, threw a wild right roundhouse punch at her. She ducked beneath it, then straightened to clap her left hand hard over his right ear. He screamed, staggered back.

She whipped a front-snap kick for his crotch. It's the easiest shot to block; reflex is hard-wired to protect the eyes and family jewels, first and foremost. Both his arms whipped down in a textbook cross block.

He'd been duped again. The woman stopped her kick without touching his treetrunk forearms, instead pivoted light on her down foot and whipped her free foot up and around to splay his nose all over his face in a squirt of blood.

He clapped his hands to his face. She wheeled a spinning back-kick into his solar plexus, then continued her turning motion to rock his head back with a roundhouse kick. Then a straight thrust-kick from her other leg drove him back into the wall with an impact that shook the building.

She danced back to stand, arms akimbo, laughing at him. Despite the pain and fury, the darkness and the lightning flashes that struggled for the honor of overwhelming his consciousness, he realized he had no chance sparring with her. Her inhuman speed—and her strength, starkly impossible in any woman, not to mention one that size—made sure of that. But he was far from a weakling, and he had at least a hundred pounds on her. . . .

He launched himself in a roaring rush, arms outstretched to seize and crush.

She stepped *into* him. Before his battered brain could respond to the unexpected move, she had caught the front of his cammie blouse and was wheeling and ducking away from him in a smooth, unhurried *aikido* move. He went sailing over her shoulder and crashed through the plywood sheeting that covered the front of the building.

He tried to scramble away on all fours, unable to hear the sound of his own sobbing through ruptured eardrums. She came through the hole he'd made like a cannonball, head tucked, arms over knees, to hit him between the shoulders and drive his face into the gravel embedded in the asphalt of the parking lot.

She straddled him, wrapped a forearm around his head. He moaned, tightened the muscles of his massive bull's neck as hard as he could. He felt his head drawn inexorably back, felt grinding squeaks from the bones of his neck. Red light flashed through his brain.

His fingers dug impressions in the asphalt. The woman grunted softly with effort. Sampson's neck snapped.

She held him a moment, grinding her crotch on his huge broad back. Then she stood, walked to the front of the former convenience store, knelt briefly to pick up an implement she'd left beside the door. A sort of C-clamp mounted on a handle, it looked like a brushhook without a blade in its jaws.

She walked to the fence. A dirt road, rutted by infrequent rain, led off across the rolling scrub. She held up a palm-sized flashlight from her utility belt, blinked it three times.

She began to hack the wire mesh with her tool. It parted like boiled vermicelli. The C-clamp jaws held a strand of wire that consisted of a single molecule, far too thin to be visible to the human eye or anything short of an electron microscope. Out in the desert motor sounds began to rumble alive.

By the time she had finished hacking a wide opening in the wire, the infrared blackout headlights of the lead vehicle of the Kirtland strike force were almost to the perimeter. She could see them as dull red beams. She waved to the driver, whose head was obscured by bizarre insect goggles, hung her tool on a special stud on her belt and walked back to the convenience store.

Zane had managed to stand up and pick his way through the hole Sampson's departure had left. He was sidling away along the front of the building on clearly rebellious legs. He looked like naughty kids had pelted him with water balloons filled with paint. Red paint.

As the column rolled into Four Hills behind her, the naked black-painted woman paused to lean over Sampson's inert body and pull his saw-backed survival knife from its belt sheath. Starlight ran cold malicious fingers along the long blade as she walked toward Zane. He pressed himself against the plywood, eyes popping from his head in terror.

She laughed. "Silly boy. I'm not going to hurt you."

She reached back to grab the collar of his jacket and pull it up. As if to give the lie to her reassurances she flipped the knife, caught it in a reverse grip, and stabbed it toward his head. He sobbed and shut his eyes.

The blade went past his ear to pin his collar to a stud that had been framed into the building front to hold the plywood sheeting. He sagged on legs that were no longer functional. The blade held him up.

"I want you to tell everyone what I did, so they will be afraid of me. I'm Misericordia. Remember that?"

He nodded. He was incapable of anything resembling speech.

"That's spelled M-I-S-E-R-I-C-O-R-D-I-A. You can call me Miseri, because we're about to get to know each other a *lot* better."

She whipped the brushhook-thing from her belt, hooked its front jaw into the top of his pants just below his navel. He produced a whimper like a stepped-on guinea pig. He'd *seen* what that thing could do.

Worse, he'd seen what the thing that held it could do.

She pulled it down. The tough synthetic fabric of his cammie pants and the skivvies beneath parted with barely a whisper. He tried to retract his scrotum into his belly.

She dropped the tool, reached inside his violated fly and pulled his cock out. It was difficult; it had shrunk to about an inch in length and was trying its damnedest to get *smaller*.

She went to her knees. "Miseri loves company, you know. And exercise always gets me fired up."

She slipped his shrunken cock in her mouth. He tensed, knowing for a fact she was going to bite it off and swallow it. Instead, she swirled her tongue around the tip, pressing back the collar of remnant foreskin, pressing on the sensitive underside.

A sweet suction began that threatened to unreel his guts through the hole in his dick. Zane had never experienced anything like that, not from his high school pep squad girl-friends, not from the skilled Vietnamese hookers who worked the southeast regardless of Councilor Brand's resolute anti-sex stand. Despite himself, he got hard in seconds.

Holding just the glans in her mouth she sucked his cock like a lollipop, jacking her fingers lightly up and down the shaft. The pleasure was incredible, so intense it momentarily overrode his fear and the gut-wrenching horror of seeing his comrades torn to pieces before his eyes.

When he was quivering on the verge of coming, she let his spit-shiny penis bounce free. He gasped. She straightened, cocked a leg around the small of his back and impaled herself on him with a scream so piercing he damned near lost the erection.

She grabbed the hair behind his ears, began pumping onto him. Her unbelievably strong leg pulled him inward on every stroke with a force that threatened to snap his spine. Incredibly she was runny with excitement; the muscles of her pussy played his cock like expert fingers.

When she put back her head and screamed again, her orgasm milked come from his cock in ropy spurts until it felt as if she were sucking all the juice from him like a spider with its prey.

The column had vanished into Four Hills. Out in the desert a light appeared. It swept forward several feet above the spring-growth grass. As it passed over the fence, the sound of shrouded rotor blades became audible, a rhythmic bass pulsation.

The verti's tilt-wing rotated vertical, and the small craft, covered in paint that reflected almost nothing in the entire electromagnetic spectrum, touched down in the parking lot. A hatch opened in the side.

A small man stood there, backlit in dim red. Incongruously, he was dressed in a white linen suit.

"Misericordia!" he snapped. "Stop that at once and come here. We're in danger of falling behind schedule."

Miseri stepped back, moaning happily as Zane's limp cock slid out of her. She kissed him on the cheek and ran lightly toward the aircraft, leaving him hanging.

The verti leapt into the sky as she shut the hatch behind her. The man in white was holding up a black halter top, bikini panties and sweat pants.

"I'm hungry," she said.

"Put these on," he commanded.

"Why should I, Dr. James?"

"Because I said to."

"But I hate to work in clothes! They cramp my style."

"You're supposed to aid the assault on Brand's villa, and I won't have you distracting Donelson's troops by running around flaunting your nakedness. Their professionalism is shaky enough as it is."

She began to pull the clothes on. He reached back and picked a matte-black weapon and a harness of spare magazines in ripstop pouches up off a seat.

"The skullcam is in its case; put it on, too. You will also take this Heckler & Koch machine pistol. It has a built-in silencer, of course. This affair is too serious for more of your bare-hand games, young lady; you've made your point."

She stuck her lower lip out. It made her look eight years old. "You never let me have any fun."

1

"Ow!" Donovan Steele jerked his head back, lowering the blue disposable plastic razor. He turned and lifted his head, examining his reflection in the mirror.

His cheeks and chin were covered with white lather that gave off nose-stinging aerosols. A swatch had been scraped clean on his left cheek. At the bottom a drop of deep red was welling out, bright against the foam.

"What's the matter?" He raised his eyes to see the reflection of Jillian Romero standing in the doorway behind him with her black hair around her shoulders and her bangs in her eyes.

He dropped the disposable razor in the sink, turned around and caught her by the arms. "I cut myself shaving! Isn't that great?"

She looked at him, then laughed. "For a minute there, I thought you were, like, weird. I guess life around you is never going to be dull, is it?"

He felt a rush of warmth for the slim, long-legged Latina. She understood almost at once why he was goofy-happy at inflicting a cut on his own face.

When she had first met him, he didn't *have* a face. He was a gleaming skeleton of polymerized nysteel alloy. The organic parts of him had long since been eaten away by the scavengers

15

of the mountains east of Albuquerque, while he lay dormant in the wreckage of his sabotaged verti.

Even before the bomb went off in his airplane, about two years ago, it had been some time since he had been capable either of shaving or cutting himself while doing so. When the functional organs that an ambush by Long Island's Borodini crime family had left him were bundled into the artificial fusion-powered skeleton Oliver Higgins had built for him, what bound it all together was bullet-resistant artificial skin that would not grow a beard or, for that matter, yield to a puny razor.

Cutting himself meant he was *human* again. Or damn near.

She hugged him. In the mirror he saw the man's white shirt she wore ride up, making very clear she wore nothing beneath it. It gave him a strange feeling.

His own daughter, Cory, would be two years older than Jilly Romero, if she were still alive.

Very lightly, Jilly kissed him on the cut, drew back with white foam on her nose and cheek and a dab of blood on her lip. "Better hurry up and get ready. The memorial services for LeRoi and the others start in half an hour. They already held them up a week while we grew your body back."

He nodded, suddenly thoughtful. She stared deep into his eyes.

"You know, they always say first impressions are lasting ones, but somehow I like these gray eyes better than those metal-type ball things you had when I met you."

He laughed, but it passed like a summer rain squall in the desert, the kind that doesn't even lay the dust but just makes big brown balls in it.

"It's Matrix," she said, quietly. "You're worried about your brother."

He nodded.

"And you're going to leave soon to look for him."

Steele said nothing.

She hugged him with surprising force, crushing her cheek against his pectoral muscles, force-grown in the Enclave vats and toned to fighting trim by electro-stimulation. "You're a man who always does what he has to. I guess that's why I love you."

She let go. "C'mon. We have to move." She turned quickly

away, but not so quickly he didn't see the sheen of tears in her brown eyes.

"We are gathered here today," Dr. Jabrandar Singh said, gripping the lectern in his brown agile hands, "to commemorate LeRoi Baraka, James Hung, Tully Roberts, Susan Mays, Edgar Delgado, Jolene Otero, Otis White, and John Sorrento, who lost their lives ten days ago while on an errand of mercy."

He raised his turbaned head and gazed out over the crowd. He was a handsome man, with a dark face and perfect beard, above middle height and very trim in his immaculate blue suit. There was a presence about him that commanded attention, that went beyond his position as head and guiding spirit of the University of New Mexico Enclave.

"They were our brothers and sisters. We shall never forget them."

The crowd murmured assent. There were perhaps two thousand residents in the Enclave, and as many of them as duty spared were gathered here on the plaza in front of Zimmermann Library to listen to their leader's voice, amplified by two balloon speakers made out of PVDF plastic that floated above his head.

Standing up front by the steps that led to the upper level on which Dr. Singh's podium was set up, Steele shifted his weight from foot to foot and surveyed the crowd. Nearby he saw plump Sally Lanz and Dave Duncan with his bearded chipmunk cheeks crying unabashedly; they had been in the ambulance crew run by LeRoi Baraka. They had been taken prisoner by the City Council in the ambush that took Baraka's life and the lives of seven young men and women from Enclave security. Jillian Romero and Dr. Singh had likewise been taken captive as part of a treacherous Council plot to lure Donovan Steele into a trap.

It had worked, too. What hadn't worked too well was keeping him *in* it.

Near Lanz and Duncan stood Cliff Sanders, a graying, heavyset black man who was head of electrical engineering at UNM. He had supported Steele when some in the Enclave wanted to turn him out, or even turn him over to the Council. Beyond him Steele recognized various men and women, for the most part painfully young, from the security contingent:

Billy Ivers, who had announced the ambush to an Enclave town meeting; big-shouldered Joe Suazo, who had commanded the security detachment at the Grand Avenue exit when Steele set out to liberate the hostages from the jail Downtown and had lent Steele an assault rifle and ammunition; Daphne Zamora, the Zuñi girl who'd given Steele her prized rocket launcher.

He heard Jilly make a noise low in her throat and laid a steadying hand on her shoulder. Steele turned. Hanging off the northern fringe of the crowd to their left, a clump of husky boys in letter jackets had gathered around big, brown-moustached Dr. Paul Houska, sociologist, former head of Social Sciences at the university, now in charge of arts & crafts and the self-anointed voice of the *sensitive* on campus. He had the look of a man who does a lot of aerobic exercise and eats a lot of bran muffins and carries around something of a gut in spite of it all.

"Backshooting son of a *bitch*," Jilly said firmly.

Steele held up a finger to shush her, squeezed her around the shoulders, marveling yet again at the wonderful warm pliancy of flesh on flesh that he thought he would never know again. "It's all right, kid. He missed."

He craned to look around the crowd. The one person he would most expect to see was nowhere in sight. She wasn't the sort to get lost in a crowd, either, unless it was a convention of retired basketball players.

There was a time, not long ago by the calender but at least two lifetimes ago by his personal chronology, when he was charging hard to maintain his well-earned reputation as the hardest-assed son of a bitch ever to wear the black of NYPD's ultra-élite Strike Force, when he would have felt total contempt for an officer who missed a memorial service for his or her fallen troops. It didn't matter what kind of afterlife you believed in, or if you believed in one at all; it was something you *did*, like saying "follow me" when going into action, like never leaving a man behind.

But now . . . maybe he could understand. A little. The officer in question was high-strung, someone he would have unhesitatingly washed out of Strike Force training as psychologically unsuited for the high-stress combat environment of Manhattan's no-man's-land. That would've been the book call, the safe call, and more to Donovan Steele's concern would have been the *smart* call. You couldn't have troops flipping out in the kill-zone; it threw their lives away and endangered everybody else. You could far less tolerate officers with too low a fracture point. The harm they could do was enormously greater.

But Janet Virág, the Enclave security chief, had what it took. She had shown that when she shot her way out of the ambush at the ancient Casa Grande motel, sole survivor of the trap that had devoured Baraka and her squad of seven and left Dr. Singh and the others captive. She had shown it when she slogged three miles against the sluggish current of the Rio Grande with a broken femur and bullets and Claymore shot in her guts to escape the heavily armed City Council gunmen.

She was cool, battle-smart, and resourceful, and most of all she was *tough*. If she hadn't been, not even the Enclave's wizard medical technology could have saved her. Despite her apparent temperamental unsuitability, Donovan Steele would've been proud—and confident—serving beside her in the Strike Force.

But she wasn't here.

Maybe it's too intense for her, he thought. *She was trashed pretty badly in the ambush. And she nurtured those kids like incubator chicks from the days right after Eruption, watched them grow from scared adolescents to a competent, battle-tested combat team. To have seven of them snuffed out in front of her eyes like candle flames. . . .*

He stopped, laughed softly to himself. Jilly looked up at him. He shook his head. She was a bright girl, with an engineer's gut understanding of how the real world worked, but this was not for her.

I'm getting tolerant. Guess this means I'm older now. And maybe I've been around the New Age types too much.

As he thought it he saw her, up on the higher level, limping slightly, her striking big-eyed face set against pain even Enclave medicine could not entirely remove. She came up to stand beside the podium from which Dr. Singh spoke. He caught her in his peripheral vision, glanced toward her, allowing a look of irritation to pass over his face.

Their eyes met. From ten meters away Steele could see understanding pass between the Enclave chief and his head of Security. Jabrandar Singh had not gotten to be one of the world's most highly regarded neurosurgeons, had not kept the Enclave together and safe for the two years of strife and deprivation that had followed Eruption, by being slow on the uptake.

Without seeming to rush, he drew the ceremony to a close, ending with a moment's head-bowed silence. For a moment the only sounds were the restless Southwest wind and the returning birds singing in the trees.

Steele moved through the quiescent crowd, not forward up the steps but to his left. Jilly came after, staying close—not because she was dependent on him, but because his bulk and calm irresistible strength cleared a path her late-adolescent slimness couldn't keep open unless she did.

Houska and his claque had their heads down, perhaps because Dr. Singh was staring right at them when he called for the silent moment. The moment ended as Steele and Jilly came up to them. Houska raised his head, yelped, and ducked behind the stocky rugby-shirted form of his ally Anne Paskoy.

"I haven't had a chance to talk to you since my last trip Downtown, Houska," Steele said.

"Haven't you done enough to him, you monster?" Paskoy demanded, sticking out her chin and her chest, both of which were formidable.

"I wasn't aware I'd done anything to him at all," Steele said mildly.

"He's been afraid of what you'd do to him since he got back," Paskoy said. "It's psychic terrorism."

"Are you sure it isn't just a guilty conscience, Ms. Paskoy?" Jilly asked sweetly. "He did try to shoot Steele in the back with a rocket launcher."

"Steele was defying the will of the community," Paskoy said firmly.

"I just wanted to tell you, Doctor," Steele said past Paskoy, "that there's no hard feelings. No harm was done either way. But please keep it in mind, I've never yet allowed anybody a *third* shot at my back."

"Threats!" Paskoy sputtered. She looked wildly around at Houska's jock coterie. "You're all witnesses!"

"I know what lies beneath that human-looking skin of yours, Steele," Houska said, emboldened by Steele's declaration of non-hostile status. "You're a killing machine. A soulless robot monster."

"I love you, too, Dr. Houska."

The most obnoxious of Houska's hangers-on, a big good-looking boy with light brown bangs hanging almost into hazel eyes, sidled over to Jilly. His name was Jeff Tillman, and he was *very* impressed by himself. "Anytime you decide to trade up to a real flesh-and-blood kind of guy, babe, you know where to find me."

She nodded. "Hanging around the locker room hoping somebody drops the soap."

Tillman colored. "The Tin Man isn't always going to be around to protect you, honey. Think about that real hard."

She reached to the small of her back. Her hand came up and around with a tiny black .380 autopistol from an inside-the-pants holster in the waistband of her cutoff shorts.

"You know the old saying, Jeffy? 'God didn't make Man and Woman equal—Colonel Smith and Colonel Wesson did.'"

He gulped and jumped back.

"A gun!" Anne Paskoy screamed. "Oh, my God!"

"Carrying a concealed weapon, eh, Ms. Romero?" Houska said. "And what do your policeman's instincts tell you about such a clear violation of the law, Mr. Steele?"

"That it's a damned good idea."

"Carrying a firearm is the right of every resident of the Enclave."

Heads turned. Dr. Singh had come down the steps. Virág was making her painful way down after him. Even Dr. Singh, a gentleman of the old school and one who was used to being obeyed, had not bothered—or dared—to offer to help the big Gypsy woman.

"I am tempted by the proposition that it is the *duty* of every Enclave citizen to carry the means of defending not just herself, but her community—an ideal you should surely find noble, Ms. Paskoy. But I understand that there are those who would resist such a measure—and I prefer not to coerce unless driven to it. Very well, Jillian, you've made your point; kindly put that thing away."

Looking not at all repentant, Jilly complied. Steele nodded to Singh. "Doctor." He didn't look at Virág, afraid of what might show in his new eyes. She was still a friend.

"Ms. Virág was kept from the memorial ceremony because she had to monitor a crisis breaking over the city," Dr. Singh said, gazing into Steele's eyes. "Her foremost duty is to the living."

"I agree," Steele said. He looked at Virág then, feeling small for having doubted her. "What's happening?"

"Shit's hitting the fan big-time. Kirtland hit Brand last night. Just flat overran her. City Council's shitting live badgers. They want to talk, plenty bad."

"To the Enclave?"

She snorted a laugh through her broken nose. "To you."

2

The Hummer stopped. Conscious that he was stepping out on the Stage of History, Colonel George Donelson climbed out and stood ramrod-straight, his riding crop held behind him. He waited, head held high to the stinging morning sunlight.

A leg extended from the light utility vehicle, encased in heavy blue cloth with a mirror-shined black shoe at the end. Out on the Four Hills' Village Green—a name that seemed optimistic, since the painstakingly tended sod had been shredded by tracks and cleated tires and churned by marching feet—sergeants bawled, "Ten-*shut!*"

To either side men in camouflaged uniforms snapped to attention. On the left the men of the 223rd Special Security Group stood proud before their armored cars, their boonie hats replaced by spiffy blue berets. To the right were the grab-bag Army types Eruption had stranded at Kirtland, less briskly erect beneath their Kevlar Fritz helmets.

In the center slumped a mass of civilians, tired and ragged, casting hunted-animal looks from side to side. When the command to stand at attention brought little response but an apathetic shuffling of feet, men in blue berets and police brassards began screaming at them.

The shock batons came out as Major General Paul Whiteman, commanding officer, Kirtland Air Force Base, returned the salute of his loyal troops. He lowered his soft black hand. The big smile on his round face slipped into a frown.

At his side Colonel Donelson shook his head slightly. The shock batons went away.

A closed camo-painted Hummer was parked nearby. It was a communications vehicle; it had the humped housing of a multiplex satellite up/downlink on the roof and a pair of camouflage-printed balloon speakers. The speakers were made of PVDF, a late-twentieth century miracle plastic, closely related to Saran wrap, that produced vibrations in response to electrical current.

An aide hustled up with a cordless microphone. Whiteman accepted with thanks.

He cleared his throat. The sound cracked out of the speakers like a gunshot. The assembled civilians cringed. Commo techs hastened to slide down the gain.

"People of Four Hills, people of Albuquerque," the general said, "welcome back to the United States of America. We greet you with open arms."

Thunderous silence greeted his words. Above the wind whistling between the former country club buildings and the palatial homes looking onto the green, an SP's snarl, "Cheer, you dumb fucks!" was clearly audible.

"We regret the necessity of employing force. I give you my pledge, we will keep the use of force to a minimum. Though we have come among you initially with guns and tanks—"

Small arms and armored cars, Donelson thought, *you sentiment-saturated wimp*.

"—realize that we have come with love in our hearts, to rescue you from the fearful anarchy that has darkened your days since Eruption."

A few of the listeners, belatedly growing hip to the fact that they were standing after all in the very eyes of the invader's guns, applauded. Whiteman beamed and glanced at his second-in-command, as if to say, *See? The kinder, gentler approach does work.*

Donelson mustered a thin smile. He had his own ideas about executive action. But the chain of command had to be respected. How else was he, Colonel George Donelson, going to reunify first Albuquerque, and then New Mexico, and then the United States of America, if not by doing everything to further the concept of *legitimate authority?* Of course, some of his notions on how to do that were decidedly unorthodox . . .

"—not our design to interfere with your everyday life," the general was saying. "We are from the government; we are here to help you. To show you that we understand your courage in facing the struggles of everyday life in the wake of Eruption, we are preparing to recognize the efforts of many of you—teachers, intellectuals, business and government leaders—in keeping your community together and viable. When I take my leave of you, my men will move among you with lists of names. If your name is on one of the lists, we will transport you to a special meeting on the future of your community and of this great, if embattled, land of ours."

A few further homilies and he concluded. The end of the general's speech was greeted with warm and enthusiastic applause. It cheered him visibly.

He walked past the communications car, holding his hand and a bright smile out in greeting to the pair who stood in front of it: a small, trim man in a white suit and Panama hat, and a slender young woman in tight black plastic pants and a colorful silk blouse, whose hair hung down her back in a long dark braid. She was munching on a ration bar.

"Congratulations," Dr. James said, shaking his hand. "Quite an inspirational speech, General."

"Thank you, Doctor. And I'd like to thank you and your assistant for all the help you've given us. Not just on my behalf, but on behalf of these people here whom you helped to liberate."

Dr. James watched Misericordia minutely as the general in turn took and shook her hand. She accepted the gesture with a firm squeeze and a Mona Lisa smile.

"We hope that our usefulness to you is only beginning—" James began, and then his "assistant" launched herself for the general in a leopard leap.

Misericordia bore the startled plump general down to the sod. The Blue Beret who had been taking advantage of his superior's turned back to lounge against the nose of the commo Hummer snapped back alert, trying to fumble his M-27 assault rifle into firing position.

There was a sound like a heavy slap. He fell back against the vehicle. The rifle dropped from his hands, its safety still on. He slid slowly downward, leaving a slug-trail of red down the Hummer's side.

"Sniper!" James yelled, throwing himself to the ground. The dropped-cinderblock thunk of the shot hit their ears.

Reluctantly, Colonel Donelson let the three fat white sighting dots of his service sidearm slip upward, away from the woman, who was trying to extricate herself from General Whiteman's flailing arms. *Interfering bitch*, he thought. He couldn't help noticing the way the thin plastic of her pants molded itself to the curve of her perfect ass like a second skin. He turned to bawl instructions to his subordinates, half of whom stood gawking and half of whom had dropped and were doing their mortal best to become one with the planet.

Misericordia got loose, grabbed Whiteman unceremoniously by his leg and dragged him behind the car as quickly as if his uniform had been empty. Another shot kicked a divot of sod loose at her heel.

"Rocket!" she commanded. The techs stared at her. Crouching in his turret, the commander of a nearby Cadillac Gage Marauder armored car shouted instructions into his vehicle's depths. In a moment an M-91 disposable launcher was passed up. He tossed it to her, then ducked down so that only his helmet and wide eyes showed.

A third shot thunked into the rear of the commo car, apparently seeking the gas tank. Moving rapidly yet without seeming to hurry, Misericordia opened and prepared the launcher, shouldered it, and stood.

As soon as she was in position she fired. Immediately she dropped flat once more. As she did a bullet gouged a bright line in the camouflage paint where she had stood half a heart-beat away.

Half a kilometer away flame shot through a second-story window of a Spanish Colonial-style villa like an incandescent white spike.

Misericordia got to her feet, smiling happily and brushing dirt from her thighs. Dr. James rolled over, sat up, and stared morosely at the grass stains on his formerly spotless Tom Wolfe suit.

"Jesus, lady," the APC commander shouted at the woman, "get down!"

Misericordia looked at him, genuinely puzzled. "Why? The sniper's dead." She took another ration bar from her pocket, peeled the biodegradable polymer wrap back, and began to eat.

3

A framed painting of a little pink-cheeked girl in a bonnet surrounded by flowers and gamboling lambs that hung on the far wall jerked away from the camera's eye. Two hands, slim and painted with flat black paint, brought a stubby H&K machine pistol into view, fired a burst left, down a blind corridor.

The viewpoint surged forward, then snapped left. Down the dark corridor, past the foresight of the H&K—now held at hip level—a man in desert cammies and matching boonie hat was holding back the trigger of a Roman-nosed Kalashnikov assault rifle in a final spasm as he fell.

"Lucky shot," murmured Councilor Tom González of the South Valley. He was a dark brown man in a linen suit and cowboy boots, possessed of a belly and a black *bandido* moustache of about equal impressiveness. He was sprawled in an uncomfortable chair in what was usually the audience seating area of the City Council chambers.

"Looks like it," agreed the voice of Dameron Crowe, chief of security for Miguel "Mike" Aragon, Council member for Albuquerque's West Side. The voice was dry and twisted. Like its owner. "But wrong again. Watch this."

The usual holographic display of the City Seal had vanished, revealing a wall-sized color LCD. On it the camera's POV was moving down the corridor in a sinuous glide, bouncing up as the camera carrier jumped over the downed rifleman, slowing as he or she approached an open door to the left.

A hand grenade flew out of the door, bounced off the flowery wallpaper above the dark wood wainscoting to the right. A black-painted hand flashed out, fielded it on the rebound, whipped it back in the door.

A crack, a flash, screams. The camera was in motion again, pivoting along with the MP barrel sticking into the bottom of the frame as it came up to the open door.

A quick image of two camouflaged figures falling, then a blurred track left. Another figure was kneeling there, seemingly undamaged by the grenade's blast or the shower of BBs it had thrown out, aiming an assault rifle.

The H&K bucked once, made a muffled sound like knuckles rapping hardwood. A red misty corona appeared briefly behind the kneeling man's head. He fell sideways, eyes staring past a tiny neat hole.

Track right, and fix on a fourth figure, cammie smock soaked in blood, face down on the floor and reaching for a fallen rifle. Another rap from the H&K. The figure's head jerked, slumped, drilled through the temple.

Abruptly the field of vision swung, stopped facing the door. A moment while the camera moved to the rhythm of slow, calm breathing.

A figure danced into view, left to right, M-27 at the hip, lips skinned back from teeth in a furious scream. No sooner had it appeared than a bullet from the H&K struck it dead center in the sternum, a clean heart shot. The dancing figure turned and fell onto its back, discharging its weapon in orgasmic spurts into floor, walls, and ceiling as random neuron firings actuated the trigger finger.

In the gloom Dameron Crowe gestured with his hand. The action froze.

"Pretty good reflexes," intoned Dino diStefano, whose district was the far Northeast Heights clear to the base of the Sandias.

"Get real, Councilor," Crowe said. He was a tiny man with a huge head and a dished face. He wore a plaid sport coat and checked pants. He leaned his slight weight on tubular crutches. "That's better than *good*. Whoever's carrying that camera *knew* where the gunner down the corridor was, and *knew* the grenade was coming, and *knew* who was still functional in the room after the grenade went off. They knew someone was making a move outside the room, and knew the exact instant they'd appear. We're talking more than just *reflexes*."

The screen went blank, back to being just an off-white bureaucratic wall. The lights came up halfway.

"Now, Dameron." It was the voice of Crowe's employer, Aragon. It didn't sound as if it was used to asserting itself. "Are you saying this, uh, gunperson is *psychic?*"

"No. But I'd guess they got damned acute hearing. True *directional* hearing. That's something animals have but we don't, along with the ability to lick their own dicks."

"You're saying the film was t-taken by some kind of *animal?*" asked Ross Maynet, the Near Heights Councilor. He was small and sleek, with blond hair thinning off a big shiny forehead promontory. Before Eruption he had been known as Albuquerque's Shoe King. Name and face recognition from his TV commercials had played a major role in winning him election to the Council.

"Superhuman is more like it."

Sitting with her long legs crossed, Janet Virág took a long drag on the cigarette she was smoking—in clear violation of any number of Council ordinances—and looked at the big black-haired man who had introduced himself as Peter Murphy.

Donovan Steele shifted in his chair. The performance had had a familiar feel to it. Had it been him wearing the microcam on the side of his head, the scene would've been played out about the same way. Only he would have used his ability to see far into the infrared to confirm with thermal imaging what his own directional sense of hearing told him about where his opponents were situated.

It was possible, of course, that the camera carrier just had combat-honed senses, a veteran's intuition as to what opponents were going to do, and superb reflexes. But his guts told him otherwise, and he trusted them. Even if this set was brand new.

"Not to be too rude or anything," Virág said, "but what has this got to do with us? What Murph and I are seeing is you people getting your ass kicked, which is basically what you deserve."

Councilor Maynet hit his feet. "This is out-out-out—I r-refuse to sit here and listen to this!" he exclaimed, spraying spit as if someone had tripped the fire sprinklers.

DiStefano tipped his big splendid head to the side. "I frequently find myself at odds with Ross," he intoned, "but I have to say, I'm behind him on this."

"Ms. Virág nearly died in the ambush you people staged at the Casa Grande," "Murphy" said. "She's still a trifle . . . emotional."

Crowe fixed Virág with a venomous glare. "Are all your brains in those mighty bazongas, babe? Do you actually think Donelson is gonna stop with just Four Hills?"

"Where is Councilor Brand now?" Steele/Murphy inquired in what he hoped was a bland voice. Murphy wore dark shades, a jacket, a shirt with a collar, and a tie. It was about as far as he could feasibly get, not just from the *Terminator* look the Councilors were all too familiar with, but from the profile of Strike Force fire-eater and rogue cyborg Lt. Donovan Steele the media had pumped into every TV set in the world. His vision preprocessors edited out the filtering effect of the shades.

The Councilors looked at one another; and then to the final member of the group. He was a tall, thin man with a yellowish cast to his features. He wore Capri pants, a wraparound silver-lamé blouse, and a bright bandanna around his hairless narrow head.

"We have her in our care." When he said *we* he meant the Crips, the swellest kid gang since the Khmer Rouge, who had taken control of downtown Albuquerque after its putative rightful owners had split for the mountains to save their butts from Eruption. He was Mr. Skin. "She is under sedation. She was quite hysterical, I fear. She kept babbling something about sheep."

Steele steepled his fingers in front of his face. "What makes you think Kirtland has the capability to threaten the rest of Albuquerque?"

González waved a big scarred hand at the blankness where the screen had been. "They kicked ass pretty good there, as your little friend with the chimichangas said."

Virág sneered and let smoke trickle from her nostrils, giving herself a decidedly demonic look. "For two years they made noises about unifying Albuquerque by force. Only now have they mustered the strength to make even this move. Sure as hell they took casualties, and it will take time and resources to consolidate their hold on the southeast part of town."

"Seems like they got a secret weapon," González said.

"Murphy" raised his eyebrows from behind the dark glasses.

"The person who took the footage we just witnessed," diStefano said. "The cameraman—or woman, if we are to believe the report we've received."

"The disc we just saw was delivered to Councilor Maynet's people under a white flag this morning," Crowe said. "At about the same time Donelson's thugs sent one of Brand's security types through a checkpoint on South Broadway over into González's territory."

"He was part of a squad guarding the perimeter out on the end of Río Arriba Lane in Four Hills," González said. "An intruder wiped 'em out. Eight men—" He snapped his fingers. "—like that. Bare handed."

"Bare more than that," Crowe said. "The witness said the intruder was wearing nothing but a coat of black cammie paint."

"Wait a minute," Steele said. "You said a *woman* did this?"

"That's right, big boy. Told the survivor she wanted to leave him alive so he could tell 'them'—translation: us—what she had done." He snickered. "Then, as the saying goes, she had her way with him. Played hide-the-salami while the strike-force convoy rolled past."

"Councilor Brand took the news badly," Mr. Skin said. "It upset her almost as badly as being forced to flee. She disapproves very strongly of sex under any circumstances, I'm afraid."

"It was rape, after all," Aragon said, wiping his forehead with his handkerchief. He kept a steady watch on Virág from the corner of his eye, and had made sure to sit as far away from her as he could without being an obvious coward. He had been the bait in the Casa Grande ambush; LeRoi Baraka's ambulance had gone there to aid him after a phony assassination attempt.

"N-nonsense," Maynet said. "A w-w-wuh—a woman can't rape a man."

"Sure we can," Virág said. "We can do a lot of things you don't give us credit for, you little bald weasel."

"She kills armed men with her bare hands. She knows where enemies are without having to see them." Crowe stood his crutches upright in front of him and rested his arms across the tops of them. "It sounds to me as if we've got a female Donovan Steele on our hands."

"Speaking of that," González said, "just where the hell *is* Steele? We asked to meet with him, not some foulmouthed broad and a yuppie."

"As I told you, I'm his representative," "Murphy" said easily. "He doesn't trust you."

"We all need to work together on this," Aragon said. Fear stood out in domes of sweat on his pudgy face.

"That remains to be seen. The City Council isn't famous for its good faith. It's well known that the only reason you don't tear each other apart is that none of you is strong enough to overpower any of the others, and you can't trust each other enough to gang up on one or two of you."

Maynet went off, but his protest drowned in saliva. DiStefano held up his hand. "Easy, now, Ross. There's nothing to be gained by arguing with these people."

He leaned forward with his hands crossed on the backs of the seats before him. "It does occur to me that you've rather put yourselves in our power. Perhaps Steele would be more . . . reasonable . . . if we were to detain you, hmm?"

"*Aji madre*," González moaned, "don't you remember what happened *last* time we tried holding hostages on this Steele dude?"

Mr. Skin reached into his shoulder bag, produced a dazzlingly chromed .357 Magnum revolver, pressed its stub muzzle against diStefano's forehead.

"Business is business, and we do profit from renting the city government buildings to you," he said. "But if you *ever* mention taking hostages from the Enclave again, I'll evacuate your skull. Your fellow Councilors will continue to pay after you're gone."

"Since you put it that way," diStefano said in a honeyed voice, "I withdraw the suggestion."

Skin made the revolver disappear. "You make my point for me, gentlemen," "Murphy" said. "Why should we trust you?"

"Because if we don't hang together, Donelson and this crazy killer bitch of his are sure as dogshit-sticks-to-your-shoes going to hang us out to dry each by our lonesome," Crowe said. "The base has been in the same boat as the rest of us: they haven't dared jump one of us for fear of extending their necks far enough for the others to chop 'em off. But now—"

He shrugged his twisted shoulders. "How long do you think the Enclave can hold out, with Kirtland armored cars right up

4

Outside the Council chambers the Councilors walked swiftly, with their heads down, eager to get away from each other and out from under the gimlet eyes of Mr. Skin's barely pubescent guards, all of whom carried guns as big as they were and looked pathetically eager to use them. Stumping painfully along on his crutches, Dameron Crowe fell behind.

"Mr. Murphy," he called.

Steele stopped, turned back.

"I just want to tell you I'm looking forward to working with you," Crowe said. He stuck out his hand.

Steele's first reaction was to wonder if Aragon's security boss had gotten into some kind of chemical mood enhancer while his back was turned. Conventional courtesy like this was completely uncharacteristic of Crowe. *Any* kind of courtesy, for that matter.

Steele was still a pretty hard-core kind of guy, but it wasn't in him to snub a dwarf. He extended his own right hand.

Crowe's face lit with evil, triumphant glee. He caught Steele's big hand in both his tiny ones and whipped it over. There, in the center of the palm, was a small disc—flesh colored, but obviously not flesh. The polymerized ceramic muzzle cover for the pistol built into Donovan Steele's right arm, in point of fact.

"So it's true," he said in a grating whisper. "You can't go around whistling, 'I Ain't Got No*body*' any more."

"How did you know?" Steele asked. He was more amused than anything else.

"Gimme a break. Look at me, Steele. I'm a crippled fucking *dwarf*, for God's sake. Also I'm ugly. And I have an attitude problem as big as all outdoors. You think I got where I am by letting stuff get by me? You carry yourself the same way whether you got meat on your bones or not, big boy. Toughest thing to fake, posture. And you super-trooper élite boys all have your own kind of special king-hell-stud walk, y'know?"

Steele looked at Crowe and saw him in a whole new light. He'd had a run-in with the little man before, when he was making his approach on the jail in Downtown where Singh and the rest were being held. He'd learned then that Crowe was sharp as the probe of a scanning-tunneling microscope, and devious as Satan.

What was only just occurring to him was that in his own twisted way, Dameron Crowe was a damned good cop. Not a straight one. But an absolute pro.

Steele glanced left. Virág stood a little way down the hall, not close enough to eavesdrop, playing buffer.

"Don't worry," Crowe said, "none of those Council drones can see past those boobs. So why the masquerade?"

Steele shrugged. "I thought so," Crowe said. "You just got this reflex where you never give anything away."

He nodded his outsized head. "I think you 'n' me are gonna get along fine."

"So what about Aragon?" Steele asked. "Are you going to tell him?"

"I never trouble the boss with facts. It only confuses the boy. Makes him feel bad."

Donovan Steele shook his head wonderingly. "This salad is *great*."

Sitting beside him, Jilly Romero looked across at her friend Angie, who had topaz eyes and a sort of fountain of chestnut hair shooting off and up from the right side of her head. Both girls burst into giggles simultaneously.

"Barf me *out*," Angie said. "The bean sprouts are all wilted, the lettuce is like *brown*, and the dressing tastes like old motor oil. This is the Student Union; the food's supposed to be cheap, not edible."

"It's what you can expect," Jilly said, "when you let New Agers grow your vegetables."

Outside the greenhouse-style glass east wall, the last pink traces of daylight had faded from the sheer face of the Sandias. Steele glanced at her and grinned. "It's been two years since I tasted anything, remember? *Anything* is going to taste good."

Angie's eyes flicked from him to Jilly, then dropped to the tofu smothered in chocolate syrup on her own plate. She shook with repressed laughter.

"Angie!" Jilly exclaimed. She turned bright red.

"Hey!" somebody shouted. "Looks who's on TV!"

Steele glanced toward the television mounted on brackets to one of the square pillars between which the redwood divider separating the food line from the dining area ran. There, against the dark hardwood paneling of his office, sat Major General Paul Whiteman, USAF, his chest aflame with ribbons and decorations, his round avuncular face shining with sincerity.

Students hooted and threw whole-wheat rolls. "Wait!" someone shouted. "Let's hear what he has to say." A hand reached up to crank up the volume.

"—reintegration of all factions of Albuquerque into the United States of America under martial law," he was saying. "Let me, as your new commander—only until such a time as fair and democratic elections can be held, let me assure you—let me be the first to say to you, welcome home."

"Some, for selfish reasons, will seek to resist this necessary step. No one regrets the use of force more than I, but I must tell you that attempts by certain parties to maintain their own rule of terror over the suffering people of Albuquerque will be dealt with most sternly. Make no mistake about this: The liberation last night of southeast Albuquerque is like unto a small pebble tossed in the ocean, but the ripples will expand outward, to cover first Albuquerque, then the state of New Mexico, and then all of what once were and what shall be again the United States of America."

With his bulky silver and purple athletic shoes propped on the stuffing-bleeding arm of the sofa in the common room of Sigma Sigma's fraternity house, a beefy jock kid with longish white-blond hair waved half a tuna salad sandwich at the wall-sized screen.

"What's he talkin' about, Jeff?" he asked past a mouthful of sandwich.

General Whiteman turned his face earnestly toward the camera. "I call upon each and every one of you to join the wave of change that's destined to sweep America."

Jeff Tillman didn't look at his friend. His eyes were locked on the screen, and they shone with reflected light.

"Keith," he breathed, "he's talking about kicking righteous *ass*."

"My friends," the general said, clasping his hands on the desk before him. "You *can* make a difference."

"Blowjob, blowjob," a voice coughed in the Student Union dining hall. Diners laughed and bounced more rolls off the screen.

"I don't know," Angie said, prodding her tofu sundae with a spoon. "If we could, like, stop all the fighting and hatred and stuff, it might be worth it. Who *cares* if the Enclave's independent—"

Steele stiffened. *That sound—*

He kicked sideways, shattered the legs right out from under Jilly's chair, caught her by the arm to ease her fall to the floor. "Everybody, *get down!*" he shouted.

He followed his own advice, throwing himself on top of Jilly, reaching under the table to grab Angie by her ankle and yank her unceremoniously out of her own chair. She yelped in surprise as her pert butt bounced on the linoleum.

"Say," she said breathlessly, "if you're getting *kinky*—"

The glass walls blew in.

The klieg lights winked out. There was a sense of deflation, as if their blinding light had been pressing outward on the walls of the office.

General Whiteman cocked his head and frowned. "What's that?" he asked. "What's that rumble?"

Standing out of the general's field of vision as well as the TV cameras', Colonel Donelson caught the eye of Dr. James and Misericordia and grinned.

"Just the four-deuce mortars at Firebase Charlie, sir," he said. "They must be taking some incoming fire. You've really made things hot for some bandit chieftains out there."

The general shook his head. "The poor people of Albuquerque. They've suffered so much, so long."

He turned to the pair from Los Alamos. "Thank you, my friends, for helping us help *them*."

Hokona Hall was burning. Flames rushed out of dormitory windows and hurled themselves into the sky like evil angels released from Hell.

Donovan Steele stood on the carefully tended lawn in front of the doomed building rubbing absently at the burn on his cheek. It hurt like a bastard, but somehow the pain didn't bother him. It reminded him of what he'd regained.

The Enclave's firefighters—volunteer, like the defense force—had stopped hosing precious water on the blaze; the dorm was a write-off. Now they were concentrating on keeping the flames from spreading to the neighboring dorms. Fortunately, the quasi-Pueblo architecture, though on the stark side to Steele's eyes, didn't offer a lot of external footholds for fire.

Dr. Jabrandar Singh sighed and threw down his bright orange wrecking bar. His white shirt was no longer immaculate, and his turban was in disarray. Like Steele and Janet Virág, the Enclave chief had been inside trying to make sure everyone within got out until the flames became too intense. They hadn't been successful; big Sally Lantz and Dave Duncan, his shoulder still swathed in bandages, were bending over the still-smoldering form of a young woman who'd jumped from the roof with her nightshirt in flames. She wasn't moving.

"I must go to the Medical Center," the doctor said. "I can do more good there as a physician."

Steele nodded. There was nothing left for him to do at all, for the moment. He hated that feeling of helplessness.

"Let me go back in, sir," he said. "The flames can't hurt me—not for very long, anyway, and there might still be survivors."

Virág gasped and clutched his arm. "No," Dr. Singh said. He nodded at the roof, from which flames were beginning to leap. "Anyone left inside there now would be beyond even our capacity to help."

He uttered a rare dry laugh. "Do not be in such a hurry to throw away the gift we gave you, Mr. Steele."

Steele nodded. He was wearied to his nysteel bones. Ultimately he was driven by a tiny fusion reactor that provided inexhaustible energy. But his vat-grown muscles—part of the "gift" Dr. Singh referred to—accumulated fatigue poisons like a normal human's.

The weariness of the body was nothing compared to the vast weight that settled on his mind. He glanced sideways at Virág, saw her face pale as the leering idiot moon that hung over the mountains, arms held stiffly down by her sides. Her hands were balled into fists, and fluid dripped from them, black in the madly dancing flamelight. It was blood; she had driven her nails into her palms.

She had a recurrent nightmare that she'd told Steele about: the big mortars at the former National Guard armory. They could reach out and touch any part of the Enclave she had dedicated her life to protecting, and there was not a damned thing she could do about it.

Tonight the nightmare had become reality, in fire and blood and whistling fragments.

"Can we withstand an attack from the base without help from the City Council?" Dr. Singh asked.

"Not a chance," Janet Virág said in a lifeless voice.

"She's right," Steele said.

"And can we trust them?" Dr. Singh asked.

"Not a chance," Virág said.

"She's right," Steele said.

5

"The battle for Albuquerque is a battle for hearts and minds."

Captain Rob Honesty, commander of Councilor Maynet's defense forces, was a two-hitch Special Forces man of the "Green Beret is Just a Hat" school. Aside from the unlikely name, he looked far too young to be a veteran of unconventional operations in Mexico and Florida, to say nothing of being a former state karate champ and lieutenant in the Serious Crimes Unit of the Albuquerque Police Department. With his fine black features, military moustache, and Errol Flynn grin he looked mostly like a male model.

Janet Virág studied her fingernails, which were cut short. "We can all see what a good job you Council boys have been doing in that line."

Honesty scowled.

"Colonel D has his own version of that saying," Dameron Crowe said. "'Grab 'em by the balls, and the hearts and minds'll follow.'"

Outside the window of the classroom in the English Department building a knot of protesters were gathered, waving placards: ENCLAVE BACK TO THE US and NO MORE WAR. Ducks paddled placidly on the pond behind the demonstrators, keeping aloof as usual from politics and proving thereby that avian intelligence is sadly underestimated. The outside attendees at

the council of war kept glancing out at the demonstrators, with
the exception of Crowe and Mr. Skin, who acted as if nothing
outside the classroom existed.

"We don't mean to contradict the wisdom of what you're
saying," the big black-haired man in the sport coat and tie
said hastily, as Honesty started to flash off. "Peter Murphy"
was turning out to be a lot more diplomatic than Donovan
Steele. "It's just that countering a main-force offensive from
the base is our main problem now. Whether Donelson can
hold onto Albuquerque once he grabs it will depend on his
winning the battle for hearts and minds. But our most urgent
task is to keep him from conquering the city in the first
place."

"This isn't going to be easy," said Gordon Walls, diStefano's
security chief. He was just under six feet tall and on the tubby
side, and wore his dark hair combed side to side over his bald
spot. He had been a beat cop once, when he had more hair
and less of the rest of him. He had been an administrator
in diStefano's organization until the Far Heights Councilor's
number-one guy, Spud Laurentian, had gotten the bright idea
of using Donovan Steele's friends as bait to draw him into a
trap. Laurentian had gotten himself and most of his command
structure wasted in the ensuing debacle. Walls had found himself
reluctantly in charge.

"The base has armor, heavy artillery, and a number of trained
soldiers. They also have their 'secret weapon' in this female
Donovan Steele."

"Speaking of Steele," said "Colonel" Carlos Camacho, who
was head of González's defense forces. He was medium-height,
with straight blue-black hair and an Indian face. He was an
authentic bad man from Chihuahua whose English, though
heavily accented, was excellent. "Just where is the dude? We've
heard so much about him."

He said that with a snide side glance toward Honesty and
Walls. When Steele had gone to Downtown to fetch his friends,
the brunt had been taken by Maynet's and diStefano's people,
and the hapless Crips, who hadn't wanted any part of the scam
in the first place.

"If your people hadn't been sniveling south of Central—"
Honesty began heatedly.

"Murphy" held up a hand. "Gentlemen, please. Lt. Steele is

reclusive. He's sensitive about his condition. You've got to consider me as speaking for him."

Camacho rolled a long black cigarillo between his hard blunt fingers. "So what qualifies you to talk war, *cuate?* You just a mouthpiece?"

"I did some work for Manny Gopir Singh in San Juan," "Murphy" said. "Might've picked up a few things along the way."

The others looked suitably impressed. The Gopir Singhs were one of the most powerful and flamboyant of the freebooter families working the Caribbean and the Florida keys.

"But how about *them?*" Camacho asked, tossing his cinderblock-shaped head at the window and the protesters clumped around. Steele recognized Anne Paskoy shouldering to the front to hold up a sign that said, SAY NO TO MURDER—STEELE MUST GO.

"Don't worry about them," "Murphy" said. "Just letting off steam."

"You can't let them go around openly questioning your commitment," Honesty said. "They'll weaken your will to fight."

"Allowing people to express themselves is kind of what we're fighting *for*," Virág said. "If we're gonna fuck around with that, I say, bag it—what's what's left for Donelson to do to us?"

Honesty shook his head. "They're potential fifth columnists. In training I saw how the Communists used people like that to weaken opposition—"

"The *who?*" Virág asked.

"Commies," Crowe said. "Twentieth century political party. Lasted maybe seventy years, then dropped clean out of sight. And good fucking riddance."

Virág frowned at Honesty. "That's ancient history. Who cares what a bunch of losers did?"

"But how can we hope to stand up to the Air Force?" Walls asked, trying to drag the conversation back to the subject by force. Despair showed in his face and voice like an infarct on an EKG.

Dameron Crowe smiled. "It's simple," he said. "We cheat."

The sixteen-year-old Vietnamese girl was thin and strikingly pretty. She wore a black silk jacket fringed in red. She was naked from the waist down; her pubic bush was brown and straight and somewhat sparse. Her thigh bled from a slash by

the Kabar knife that had been used to cut off her panties and
red-trimmed black trousers.

"Come on, baby," Orvus crooned, flicking blood from the
tip of his knife. "You gonna give it up *so nice*."

She turned to run. A booted foot tripped her up. She fell
sprawling in the rubble of what had been a beauty parlor before
the four-deuce mortars of Fire Base Charlie—the National
Guard armory on Wyoming—had given this block of East
Central a good going-over.

Barbara Brand's domain wasn't pacifying according to plan.
Though the Security squaddies didn't know it, earlier that
day and halfway across town Dameron Crowe had adequately
summed up Colonel Donelson's philosophy on subject peo-
ples. If the Southeast Albuquerqueans didn't want to comply
with the new rule, they'd serve as damned fine examples to
the rest of the city as to the cost of defying Reunification.

Boom-Boom and Jammer went to their cammie-clad knees,
pinning her hands in the rubble. The girl flailed her bare legs.
"Shit!" Jammer exclaimed. "Bitch won't hold still."

"Who wants a piece that's lyin' still?" Orvus asked, unsealing
his trousers. He pulled them down to his knees. After the fashion
of line troops he wasn't wearing underwear, a rigid pink banana
arc. His cock snapped out, a rigid pink banana arc.

He stuck the knife blade-down in the rubble and grabbed
her flying knees. "All *right*, little darlin'," he said, grunting
with the effort of pressing her legs out flat to the sides. "Get
ready for Papa." He leaned forward.

His collar jerked taut like a noose around his neck. He was
yanked to his feet and spun around. His cock waved wildly
in front of him.

"What the—fuck?"

His voice trailed away. A giant black shadow loomed
between him and the sun. He smelled cigarette smoke.

"Lookin' for a hot time, big guy?" Janet Virág said. She
puffed her cigarette to a furious glow, took it from her mouth,
and pressed the live ember to the tip of Orvus' cock.

Orvus screamed and went down jackknifing and thrashing
in the debris. Boom-Boom, Jammer, and the captive girl were
all frozen by the unexpected turn of events.

Jammer, to the captive's right, came out of it first. He spun
around, caught his M-27 GI assault rifle by the sling, leapt to

his feet. He came around trying to fumble the pistol grip into
his right hand.

The tall woman stood there laughing at him. He gaped,
unable to comprehend why she wasn't reacting, going for a
weapon, or cringing in fear. Didn't she know he had a *gun?*

"Look down, ass-white," she said.

He glanced down. His camouflage blouse was open almost
to the navel; he wore a tan tee-shirt beneath it. Dancing on his
sternum was a dot of ruby light, dim in the sunlight.

As he watched, dust puffed from the tee-shirt, followed by
a spurt of blood. His eyes met Virág's in a look of pure
astonishment. He fell.

Boom-Boom had seen enough. He jumped to his feet and
ran, elbows pumping, untucked tails of his cammie blouse
flapping.

Virág swept her right hand down, popping the safety strap
of her Kevlar combat holster with the pinkie finger. Her fingers
closed around the butt of the big replica Desert Eagle .44 Mag.
She hauled it out, straightened her arm, fired freehand.

Boom-Boom stumbled as a shot took him in the center of
the back. As he pitched forward a second caught him square
in the back of his head and blew his face over a stub of
cinderblock wall.

Groveling in the dust by Virág's right boot, Orvus found
the hilt of his Kabar with his shoulder. Pain was crowded
from his mind by a bright red vision of vengeance. He seized
the weapon, plucked it from the hard earth and struck like a
scorpion for his tormentor's leg.

Virág whirled. Her shot and the shot from Steele, covering
her from a former porn shop across the street, hit the soldier
simultaneously, rolled him onto his back with dead eyes and
dick pointed at the futile sky.

Virág crouched beside the girl, who was curled into a fetal
ball, weeping soundlessly but so violently she seemed likely
to shake herself to pieces. Taking her huge pistol in both
hands, she scanned her surroundings, in case the late great
trio's buddies happened to be in earshot.

"*You're clear, Janet,*" Steele's voice said in her ear. The
words were transmitted by a tiny PVDF mike that looked for
all the world like a round Band-Aid taped over his larynx,
bounced by a smart phased-array transceiver the size of an

electric razor to a Raytheon Jakarta satellite in geosynchronous orbit, and back down to a similar unit buttoned into Virág's cammie blouse and thence to a bone-conduction speaker taped behind her ear. It was a long way around for a call from across the street—about 36,000 miles out of the way, round trip— but it was at the speed of light, static free, and with very little chance of interception. Beat hell out of just shouting across Central.

"I hear you," she subvocalized; you didn't even have to talk out loud for the little wonder mikes. Just go through the motions.

She holstered her sidearm, gently took the girl by the shoulder. "Come on with me, honey. You're safe now, but you're gonna have to move if you want to stay that way."

"—see what Kirtland's 'pacification' really means," the young woman said to the videocam. Behind her, Virág picked the half-nude girl up, set her on her feet, and began to urge her across Central. "Enclave forces were able to intervene in time to save this young woman from rape and probable murder. But who knows how many more people are being victimized back there in the rubble—and how many more will suffer before Colonel George Donelson ceases his campaign of naked aggression?

"This is Jilly Romero, KUNM News."

Hector Sandoval lowered the camera from his shoulder and hunkered back behind the fragment of wall from which he had filmed the proceedings across the street. Another portable satlink antenna, this one in a backpack resting on the cinder-strewn floor of the half-wrecked storefront, had bounced the scene to the KUNM studios, which had relocated on-campus after Eruption, for rebroadcast to the city at large.

"Jesus, Jilly," he said. "I can't believe you're gonna show the whole thing."

She had already crouched out of sight of the street. She peeled her lips back from her teeth. "It's reality. We want the people of Albuquerque to see what this benevolent outreach crap of General Whiteman's really amounts to. And what they're up against."

"But don't you think Jan was, uh, kind of *hard* on those guys?"

Jilly blinked at him. "No."

"*Vehicle coming*," Steele's voice said in her bone-conduction speaker. "*Hummer running heavy. Probably friends of the deceased.*"

She gestured at the other two members of her crew. "Chris. Pati. Go help Ms. Virág get the girl in the van. It's time to book."

6

"Convoy come, man."

Baby Gaby was about four feet tall and his headband all but entirely hid his twelve-year-old eyes. He held his Mexican imitation of an early twenty-first century bullpup Galil with authority, though, and his skinny body slipped through the nighttime rubble like smoke. Rob Honesty had worked with worse.

Off west across the river a volcano rumbled and farted with a noise like God's own satchel-charge cracking off. Despite himself Honesty winced. When the sensory package said *incoming*, reflex tended to take command. Nobody noticed; his ambush party had all been ducking too, even the ones who'd never been under artillery fire in their lives. The volcanoes had created reflexes of their own.

He snapped down his IR goggles. South on six-lane-wide Wyoming had been a river of blackness without them, with vagrant gleams reflected from dead-vehicle chrome and glass that survived in derelict storefronts. Now it lit up eerily red and vivid with the infrared beams of the Kirtland vehicles.

By sundown yesterday scouts had reported that Donelson's troops had occupied the southeast quadrant of town as far north as Lomas and as far west as Wyoming. Fire Base Charlie was no longer an outpost, but the cornerstone of their perimeter.

Donelson was still concentrating on consolidating his hold on Southeast Albuquerque. A few skirmishes aside, his men had made no aggressive moves since the 4.2-inch mortar barrages that followed General Whiteman's televised call for the city's surrender, striking all the holdout sectors in turn, starting with the UNM Enclave.

Wyoming for much of its length served as the border between the territory ruled by diStefano and the dominion of Honesty's employer, Ross Maynet. That made it a no-man's-land, and Kirtland had always been fairly arrogant about running patrols up and down it, as if to show what they really thought of the military capabilities of the rival Council members. *We can take you any time*, they seemed to say, and *any time* had finally arrived.

Two days ago—about the time the Council had been meeting with the people from the Enclave—a patrol had probed far enough north to come in sight of the southern perimeter of the Albuquerque Academy, the former private school diStefano had made over into his fortress. No shots had been exchanged, but the academy compound had been thrown into a panic. Since that time base armored columns had driven up and down Wyoming at will.

Time for a change, Honesty thought. He grinned.

He had a platoon, of sorts. Three squads of roughly twelve men each, one from the Crips and one from diStefano's Far Heights added to his own Near Heights contingent. The unit had hastily been cobbled together as part of the new anti-Donelson alliance. It was maybe not an ideal arrangement, but he thrived on it; working with wild-ass indiges was what he'd been trained for, after all.

Hunched over, he moved south along the facade of an old Black Angus steak house, restored after the New Mexico legislature legalized meat-eating again a few years before Eruption. The railroad tie and poured-cement planters that ran along the front of the building provided excellent cover and concealment. He had the Crip squad with him here on the east side of Wyoming, and strung out into the parking lot north and south. The unit's median age seemed to be about fifteen, and the kid gang members had a proclivity for grab-assing and making noise, which was why he'd wanted them under his own eye.

Once he'd made clear that he wasn't taking any back-chat and would lay out anybody's ass he had to, they had begun to pay attention to him. Now with the engine noise of enemy vehicles rising like a wind from the south, they became businesslike and still, blending into the shadow as if the night were their natural environment.

As along most of its length, Wyoming was basic Strip Mall Hell here, where it crossed a major east-west artery called Menaul. The Menaul intersection was a basic red zone. About two weeks ago, just before the fiasco in Downtown, the Great Satans motorcycle club had bushwhacked a Kirtland patrol at the crossing. The commander of the approaching column would definitely have ambushes and snipers on his mind.

There was about a fifty percent chance he'd decide to put the pedal to the metal and bust through the intersection at full speed, hoping to clear the jaws of any trap before they could close. The other, equal possibility was that he'd slow way down so that he could make the crossing in a rolling overwatch, one vehicle stopping to cover while another leap-frogged past to cover from a more advanced position.

"*Rob, Watts.*" It was the voice of his second in command, who had the Near Heights contingent belly down in the strip mall west across Wyoming, which like the Black Angus sat right up against the street, forming a choke point before the terrain widened out again into parking lots to meet Menaul. "*They're slowing, over.*"

"I read you, Danny," he subvocalized. "All right, every-body. Wait for my word. I say again, wait for my word. Honesty out."

The column was contracting like an accordion. Honesty wanted to pump his fist and shout *yeah!* in triumph. This was ideal, the enemy bunching in the kill zone. And even if they weren't, if the coin flip had gone the other way and they blazed on through. . . .

Honesty unslung his grenade launcher. It carried a drum mag of 30mm grenades behind the pistol grip and was capable of full-auto fire. Around him the Crips were prepping their half-dozen M-91 launchers. He'd run them through the drill before coming on this sortie, expecting to have to run a quick clinic with lots of patience. But they handled the light AT rockets like pros. It gave him a new angle on exactly why his employer and his fellow Council members hadn't tried reclaiming Downtown by force.

The lead car drew abreast of Honesty's position, a Marauder with the long probe of a 25mm automatic cannon testing the night ahead. Behind came a second armored car with a stubby automatic grenade launcher that fired 40mm rounds which carried more punch than his own hand-held 30s did, mounted beside a .50-caliber machine-gun. Next came a six-wheel truck with a squad of troops packed under a Kevlar shell, and a Hummer carrying a rollbar-mõunted machine-gun. A third Marauder with side-by-side 40mm and .50-cal brought up the rear.

Serious firepower, Honesty thought, and smiled. It was a lot of men and matériel, all neatly packaged for destruction.

"Ready?" he asked the night. Whispered assents answered him.

"All right. First squad, rock and *roll*."

Four missiles hissed from the east side of Wyoming. *Not bad*, he thought. The first volley was supposed to be three, but one overeager indige rocketeer wasn't bad. Not bad at all.

Two missiles hit the lead car with the ear-piercing *crack* of HEAT rounds going off. The car veered to the left, ran over the median, then over the far curb to run down into the sunken parking lot and ram a light pole. It stopped.

Another missile hit the turret of the trail car. The Marauder kept moving, but a hideous white glare shone through the small hole the shaped-charge warhead had made. The final rocket went to Jesus; Honesty never even saw it hit.

The idea had been to send the first volley downrange, one missile to an armored car, with the second three saved for follow-up shots as needed. Still, three solid hits on two Marauders was damned fine shooting for the real world.

Honesty stood up and fired the grenade launcher from the hip. The twenty rounds in the drum were all High Explosive, Dual Purpose grenades, basically small shaped-charge projectiles. They had an outside chance of defeating the foamed-metal armor of the Marauders.

They had an *excellent* chance of messing up the six-by, however. Honesty saw the interior of the truck's cab light up hellish white as spikes of incandescent copper shot through the door, and fancied he heard the driver scream. He walked the burst back along the Kevlar shell. The plastic armor provided enough resistance to set the tiny warheads off, and the HEAT charges burned through like a bad boy taking a hot needle to his plastic models.

The six Crips who didn't carry launchers had opened up with assault rifles. The three crewmen in the machine-gun-armed Hummer were dithering as rounds began to crack past their ears. The second Marauder in line stopped, its one-man turret traversing right to bear on the Black Angus.

The troop truck ran into the rear of the ten-ton armored car. Soldiers were spilling from the back, some with uniforms on fire, rolling down the slope into the parking lot on Wyoming's west side.

Honesty blazed the last of his mag at the Hummer without scoring apparent hits. "Second Squad, do it to it," he said, and dropped behind a planter.

The sunken lot lit up as Claymore mines concealed among windblown clumps of trash went off with a rippling roar. Kirtland soldiers screamed as they blew away on a high-velocity wind laden with steel shot.

"All squads, fire at will."

The turret blew right off the lead Marauder on a column of blinding yellow fire. The Crips' last two M-91s neatly bracketed the turret of the second armored car, rocket flames drawing bright lines through the night. The crew decided they'd had enough. Cleated tires gouged asphalt as the car backed over the median, turned its nose south, and gunned it with rifle fire sparking along its sides.

The Hummer was already beating cheeks back to Fire Base Charlie. The final Marauder in line had run its right tires up on the sidewalk just south of the steak house. Its turret hatch had been blown off by a crackling fireworks show as the ammo for its two weapons cooked off. Its crew was desperately ditching, more willing to face the ambushers' bullets than the flames.

It was a perfect ambush. Absolutely textbook. If they hung on for a few moments more, they could waste every last soul who wasn't in the two vehicles that were rapidly receding into the south. But Dameron Crowe, that weird and twisted little geek, was agitating for prisoners and more prisoners to question. Honesty had seen some pretty scaly things in Central America and the Keys, but he had a feeling he did not want to know exactly what Crowe intended to *do* to them. But he knew perfectly well they could never have too much information about their enemy's capabilities and intentions. . . .

Rob Honesty said, "Cease fire. Pull back now and make for rendezvous. I say again, it's time to boogie. Go, go, *go*."

The National Guard armory wasn't even supposed to *have* four-deuce mortars. In the initial years after the war the country had undergone a force contraction, as the government pulled much heavy equipment and many troops back East to defend the largest surviving population centers—and, not incidentally, the new seat of government.

Later, when the status of secessionist Texas had been in doubt, the new national government in midtown Manhattan had none-too-subtly stripped New Mexico of even more matériel to prevent it falling into Texan hands. The Easterners who ran what was left of the country didn't quite realize that New Mexicans and Texans are not exactly natural allies, even though the breakaway Republic was a far different creature from the belligerent big neighbor that had tried repeatedly to annex New Mexico by force in the days before statehood, and ever after had sent invasions of beer-swilling, loud-mouthed tourists with pointy-toed, lizard-skin boots and ten-gallon hats on half-pint heads to bedevil them each year.

Finally, most of what little heavy equipment remained out West had been stripped for fights against the surlier Freebooters—and the well-armed gangs of Manhattan's no-man's-land. Trouble had begun to break out in Albuquerque, among other places, but it was deemed—from the vantage point of Manhattan—to be small-scale civil disobedience, best dealt with by small arms and armored cars.

Fire Base Charlie's four 4.2-inch mortars were fairly heavy ordnance. A concerned CO with an eye to the future had preserved them by writing one off from battle damage, another from nonreparable malfunction, and bribing a programmer to jimmy the database to simply lose the other two. The available stocks of ammunition of various sorts were condemned as unsafe by reason of advanced age, with the help of a little further jiggering of computer records. The enterprising commander had even managed to cadge more 4.2-inch ammo for several years by the simple expedient of requisitioning it; when, years later, Manhattan noticed and demanded that Albuquerque send back the rounds it had received for its "nonexistent" mortars, the CO's equally quick-witted successor had promptly condemned the later shipments too.

The mortars were set up inside a twenty-meter circle in the middle of the compound, with buildings masking them to the north and west—fortuitously the two directions attack was most likely to spring from in the current scheme of things. The tubes were additionally protected by head-high sandbag ramparts. It wasn't an optimum arrangement from the standpoint of safety, but the current thinking was, against enemies who lacked aircraft or appreciable artillery assets of their own, the benefits in laying and loading the pieces outweighed the risks entailed in bunching them.

Since the invasion of southeast Albuquerque, the mortars had been going day and night, practically without pause. When the panicked call came from a convoy that had fallen in deep shit just up Wyoming, nobody thought anything of it. They just retrained the pieces and let 'em rip.

"Now I know how Matrix feels."

Just shy of a kilometer to the northeast, Donovan Steele stood on the blacktop of a middle-school yard, buckled from below by the inexorable pressure of weeds growing. He had his arms folded across his chest, a look of concentration on his face, and a thin cable running out of the hair at the back of his head to a console set beside him on the asphalt.

Jilly and a skinny kid genius from the UNM math department named Epstein, who had thick glasses, frizzy black hair, zits, and bad teeth, were monitoring figures that danced on a folded-up, self-luminous liquid crystal display.

She reached out to touch Steele's hand, quickly, almost furtively. "You worry about him, don't you?"

He nodded.

"What could happen to him? Nothing could harm him, could it?"

"I don't know," he said. "Right now I have other things to worry about."

The heavy artillery of the Free Albuquerque Alliance—that was what Jilly called it anyway, and whoever had started it, the name seemed to be picking up currency—rested on the

pavement nearby. Three 82mm mortars, runt brothers of Fire
Base Charlie's four-deuces, with shorter range and a puny
fraction of the punch. It would be suicidal presumption to
think of stacking them up against the battery of bigger mortars.
Except. . . .

A whistling, rushing roar like a passing train mounted in the
sky. Steele tracked it with his head as it arced high, rolled over
the top to the west of them, and began to scream down. North
and very slightly west of them a white flash lit the sky.

Steele had his head turned southwest again before the subway rumble of the barrage hitting home vibrated up through
the soles of their feet, which were showing a tendency to
stick to the asphalt, still slightly gummy from the day's spring
desert heat.

"Got a good fix?" Jilly asked, all business now, peering
intently at her screen. "Numbers look solid here."

"I got a fix."

Jilly was an exceptionally bright, cute girl just starting
to come out of adolescence. She was also a fine fledgling
engineer, with an engineer's eye for the practical. When Dr.
Eleanor Ngoya and her gnomes at the Med Center had regrown
Steele's body for him, Jilly had them implant a non-allergenic
socket at the back of his head, to permit him to jack directly
into one of the general-purpose input/output ports the builders
had put in his nysteel skull.

Steele had tracked the four-deuce salvo with his highly directional hearing and with his eyes, his infrared vision enabling
him to pick up the glow air friction raised on the projectiles as
they raced toward their rendezvous with the planet. Following
them through half their arc had given him a very exact fix
on where they'd come from, which he was then able to feed
directly to Jilly and Epstein and their homebrewed fire-control
computer. They in turn fed figures to their own mortar crews,
under the direction of a grizzled, swag-bellied old artilleryman
who'd spent the last ten years working as a welder in the South
Valley, which was now Tom González's turf.

The welder nodded. The crewfolk dropped rounds down the
three small tubes.

The three 82mm rounds cracked off just outside the defensive rampart, one of them hitting the piled bags.

The crew chief stared in horror at the whirling plume of sand. He spun, grabbed the nearest mortarman by the front of his blouse. "Fire up the counterbattery radar!"

The man gaped at him. "How?"

The AI subroutines at play beneath the conscious level of Donovan Steele's mind processed the sounds of the first barrage hitting and fed corrections to Jilly's board. The welder scratched at where his web belt was chafing the overhang of his gut, spat tobacco juice, and made minute adjustments.

The next volley was fired for effect. It consisted of white phosphorus rounds, the dread Willie Peter. They dusted everything within the defensive ringwall of sandbags with flecks of metal that clung like ticks—to faces, hands, and several hundred mortar rounds stacked in their plastic crates—and burned at a temperature of 2700° Centigrade.

The second round was Willie Peter too. Dameron Crowe, who'd helped cook up the scheme for neutralizing the armory's dreaded four-deuce battery, had insisted on it. Jilly's mouth was compressed to an almost invisible line in the starlight. She had agreed with the necessity of using WP, knowing she would have to live with the knowledge of what she was doing to the unseen mortarmen.

The third volley was high explosive. By the time it whoomped on its way the Alliance crew could hear an almost constant rattle of secondary explosions.

Only Donovan Steele could hear the screams.

7

Colonel George Donelson reared back from the holographic display map table. Its polychrome glow underlit his face, giving him a demonic appearance.

"What do you mean?" he demanded. "I say we need to hit the Enclave first. Hard and fast. That's the way to go."

Misericordia folded her arms under her small breasts and turned away, looking bored. She wore a loose silk blouse, a wraparound skirt, and a gaudy bandanna wound around her long dark brown hair.

Dr. James faced the colonel's bluster without a flicker of expression crossing his features. They were drawn, pale, ascetic features, the features of a monk, an artist, a holy madman.

"Striking first at diStefano offers you the chance to score a knockout blow on one of your opponents; your own intelligence reports that their defensive forces were effectively decapitated during that imbroglio Downtown. It gives you a chance to fracture the Alliance. And finally, it offers far shorter lines of supply than an attack on the Enclave does, while, if it's successful, it will at the least eliminate a potential threat to the flank of any thrust at the Enclave—considerations I should think you would have found elementary, as a military man."

Donelson's face contorted, reddened. "God damn it, I don't need amateurs—"

General Whiteman held up a soft black hand. "George. Please." He looked at the white-clad scientist with his doe's eyes. "Why should an attack on diStefano jeopardize the bandit Alliance, Doctor?"

"The Far Heights lie at Albuquerque's easternmost extent. Only Maynet's territory abuts it. The others must send their troops a good long ways to reinforce—while we enjoy the advantage, to which again I should think the colonel would not be insensible, of being able to operate along interior lines against Maynet, the Enclave, González, and the Crips."

James produced a thin smile. Or at least a twisting of the mouth suggestive of a smile. "The rest of the Alliance might think long and hard about how severely they desire to expose their own people—and weaken their own defenses—to haul the fat of a bitter and unscrupulous rival out of our fire. Which ought, in turn, cause them to consider how much they can rely on their supposed allies' faith."

Collecting himself, Donelson settled back in his chair. He managed to calm the waters of his face behind his moustache. Internally he seethed. *What do these damned civilians know about* anything? He had so many objections inside that he had to keep his mouth shut for a moment for fear they'd all come spilling out at once as unintelligible babble.

Control, he told himself. *If you can't master yourself, you can't master America*. He couldn't let the general think he was losing it. Whiteman had power over him, Whiteman could relieve him. Soft, weak, womanish Whiteman . . . it was intolerable. But the time was not right to change it.

"I thought your big priority was apprehending Donovan Steele, Doctor," he said, pleased at how steady his voice held. "He's in the Enclave, in case you've forgotten."

"If it looks as if we're about to overwhelm diStefano, Steele will appear." James steepled pale fingers before his eyes. "You may take my word for that."

"But if, as you suggest, Doctor, the attack on diStefano splits or weakens the Alliance," Whiteman said, "won't the Enclave be reluctant to send aid?"

Misericordia lowered her hands, brushing the front of her skirt into a brief rustle of motion, momentarily baring a flash of pale thigh. Donelson swallowed audibly.

"All the more reason he'll be there," she said in her slightly throaty contralto. "He'll feel honor bound to help, no matter what anybody says or does. Donovan Steele is an honorable man."

James reached out and patted her hand. "The girl is only a few months old, chronologically, though she is in her early twenties biologically," he explained. "She's a child in many ways, with a child's naïve notions."

He shrugged slightly. "Still, she has a point. This is how I believe Steele will respond. And while the Enclave—Steele aside—has by far the weakest offensive capabilities of any rebel faction, they have the strongest defenses. Steele will be a tough enough nut to crack without the Enclave's defensive shell around him. Striking diStefano gives us the opportunity to draw Steele out."

Donelson glared daggers at James, who didn't even look at him. The general sat for a long moment with his head sunk to his chest. Then he nodded.

"You are very persuasive, Doctor. You've sold me; we shall concentrate our forces in an initial offensive against diStefano."

Donelson blew air explosively through his nostrils. He glared at James and his bitch-in-heat test-tube killer through slitted eyes. *You're outliving your usefulness a lot sooner than anticipated*, he told them silently.

Whiteman wagged his head sympathetically at his subordinate and turned to Misericordia.

"You seem to possess compassion for this Lieutenant Steele, possibly even admiration," he said. "You want to take him into custody so that you can help him, rehabilitate him—is that it?"

"Oh, no, General," Misericordia said, and smiled angelically. "I want to kill him."

The Kirtland forces struck in the gray before the sun had rolled up from behind the bulk of the Sandias. Their heavy artillery—the four-deuces of Fire Base Charlie—were written off as irreparable, legitimately this time. But they had an abundance of lighter 82mm mortars, as well as shoulder-fired rockets, primarily M-91s, with AT and high-explosive warheads. They also possessed a number of very potent direct-fire weapons, from the quick-firing twenty mike-mikes and 40mm grenade launchers on their armored cars on down.

A rolling barrage of 82mm rounds and HE rockets roused the Far Heights defenders dozing at their posts. It was followed by Marauder armored cars bombing straight north up Juan Tabo, closely supported by troops in Kevlar-covered trucks and Hummers.

Some of diStefano's stalwarts took to their heels or broke down completely, cowering in the rubble at the sound of the artillery slamming down around them; even light artillery is no fun, especially for sporadically trained, unseasoned troops.

But there had been plenty of action to go around in Albuquerque since Eruption; not all the troops were green and easily spooked. DiStefano's people had motivation on their side, too. They were defending their homes—or their stake in diStefano's pie, depending. And they had seen all too vividly what occupation by the troops of the 223rd Special Security Group meant, thanks to the risky and incessant efforts of teams of KUNM video newskids infiltrating the captive Southeast.

Heavy artillery might have been a rarity in North America, outside the Eastern Seaboard, the Keys, and Texas, but shoulder-fired hardware was commonplace. Defenders dug into buildings and yards slammed the onrushing armored cars with whining volleys of M-91s—cheap knockoffs from Mexico, actually, but capable of messing up a Marauder when you bounced enough off it.

Donelson's Red Army tactics cost him lots of armored cars. He had plenty. When rockets buzzed toward the cars, the infantry came spilling out of their vehicles and went into action, surrounding and snuffing pockets of resistance. Superior training and discipline did tell, as Donelson thought it would; toe to toe in the rubble, diStefano's semi-guerrilla army was no match for Kirtland troops, either 223rd or Army.

Sometimes the defenders stood off the infantry, confidence reinforced by strongpoints of cement and sandbags. When they hit those, the base troops held back and called for tear and nausea gas. If that didn't bring the defenders weeping and puking out into the watery light of overcast day to be shot down, the hard stuff came on: flame weapons—napalm rockets and scratch-built flamethrowers—and for busting serious bunkers, direct-fire optically guided missiles capable of splitting the toughest main battle tank open like a potato in a microwave, weapons that packed far more punch than even the lamented four-deuce mortars.

Donelson's hard-charging spearhead drove deep into the Far Heights, leaving its casualties burning by the way.

"I'm not going," Janet Virág said.

Donovan Steele stared at her across the table, unable to believe he had heard her correctly.

"I won't do it. Dino diStefano has already tried his best to kill you—and me and Dr. Singh and your little pal Jilly too, for that matter." She tossed her dark hair defiantly back over broad shoulders. The fluorescent overhead lights of the fifth-floor lounge in the University Medical Center turned the red-gold highlights at the ends of her hair an eerie pallid green.

Steele felt his hands knotting into fists. "So you're planning to leave our allies high and dry."

Her eyes blazed. She controlled herself with visible effort. "Listen, *gad*—Donovan. The base is aiming a knockout blow at the Far Heights. For us to try to lend a hand would require driving halfway across town, with Kirtland troops on one flank and Maynet on our left. We'd just be begging to be cut off and chopped up."

"Why not an attack into territory held by Kirtland closer by?" Jilly Romero asked. She was sitting while Steele paced. "We might be able to distract them. Maybe we could, like, do some serious damage, if they really are putting everything into this attack on diStefano like you say."

Virág started to give her one of those "if I feel the need for an unqualified opinion, I'll beat it out of you" looks. Sitting at the head of the table looking as immaculate and cool as if he'd just been put on display at Madame Tussaud's, Dr. Singh cleared his throat. For a man who possessed a really bewildering array of credentials, he was anything but credential conscious; anyone could say anything in his presence, Steele had noticed, as long as it made sense. If it didn't, no string of degrees was going to preserve your ass from the chewing the doctor would give it in that same calmly meticulous manner in which he did everything.

Jilly was making sense. "We don't have a lot of offensive clout ourselves, *Ms.* Romero," Virág said. "Donelson's holding back mobile reserves that can contain anything we can throw at him, including your big bad boyfriend."

"We've got a commitment to Councilor diStefano," Steele said, fighting to keep his voice level.

Virág looked at him, blew smoke through her nose. "Honey, what we got here is a basic conflict. Yeah, the Enclave has a commitment to diStefano. But I, personally, me, Janet Virág, as head of Enclave security, *I* have a commitment to protect and serve the Enclave. At any cost."

She took a hit off her cigarette. "I've put my ass on the line regular—in fact I just got it blown off and regrown; the dimples on my pink and shiny new butt haven't even set yet. No biggie. Neither is my life, y'know? So if this whole thing costs me my honor—" She shrugged.

"I'm going," Steele said. "I'll ask for volunteers, but I'll go by myself if I have to."

"I'm going too," Jilly announced promptly. Virág narrowed her eyes.

"No," Steele said. "It's out of the question."

"Oh, bullshit," Jilly said. "What am I, some delicate little flower who's only good for getting into trouble and needing to be rescued?"

Steele showed her the shadow of a grin. "You've needed rescuing once or twice, that I can recall."

"*¡Coño!*" Jilly said.

"Take anyone who'll go with you, Steele," Virág said. "Fuck, take 'em all, if they'll go. But remember. You take every last swingin' dick and bouncing titty I got to my name, it still won't be enough to pull diStefano's hairy chestnuts out of the fire. And every one who leaves the firing line here makes it that much more likely he ain't gonna have a home to come back to—if he survives."

Steele stood staring down at her. She sat looking up at him, half-sprawled now, deceptively lazy as a tigress in the sun, giving away a height advantage she could almost have nullified by simply standing.

She was right, too. Every word she said—right down to her first commitment being to the Enclave.

To protect and serve, she had said. He had lived those words himself. Had lived literally behind them, engraved on the badge he wore as a member of the New York City Police

Department. Had lived them until he was literally blasted and burned out from behind them in a Borodini crime family ambush, and beyond, as a cyborg, even as a fugitive hunted by his brother officers. Had lived the words until they wouldn't let him live them any longer.

He looked at the head of the Enclave. "Dr. Singh?"

"I cannot forbid you. I have no power over you. Neither will I order Ms Virág to assist you. I have charged her with maintaining the security of this Enclave because I feel she is best for the job. I cannot override her unless I am prepared to replace her. I am not so prepared, Mr. Steele."

"But what about the Alliance? DiStefano is relying on us."

Singh spread his long strong surgeon's hands. "You may call for volunteers."

Steele stood for a long moment. "Okay. Okay, I will."

Jilly rose. He turned and left.

The wind had come up with afternoon. Misericordia stood with her long skirt whipping around her slim legs eating apples from a big burlap bag and gazing moodily at the charred and torn remnants of the 4.2-inch mortar emplacement. It looked as if a fresh volcano had erupted through the pavement of the armory complex.

To one side Colonel Donelson sat in his Hummer with his arms folded on the dash and his head rested moodily on them. To the other a verti painted in a tan speckled snake pattern was parked, its wings rotated vertically, its curved black polymerized graphite propellers quiescent. Dr. James sat on a folding lawn chair between the colonel's personal vehicle and his commo car, a disturbingly white Panama hat shading his eyes, reading a satlink-downloaded copy of the British science journal *Nature* and sneering.

Misericordia stiffened, looked north and east, then crossed her arms and smiled a secret smile.

Several minutes later a tech came boiling out of the commo Hummer as if he'd kicked over a yellowjacket nest inside it. "Colonel Donelson!" he bawled, hopping to attention next to his commander's car and snapping a salute that cracked like a whip. Like any self-respecting guy with the sense to catch a job in the rear with the gear he knew what to kiss and when.

Donelson raised his head. "Well? Spit it out, man, I don't have all day!"

"Colonel, sir, Captain Logan reports a probing attack on his left flank, out of Councilor Maynet's territory. Main axis of advance seems to be along Constitution. It's almost to Juan Tabo, sir; the captain reports it's, ah, 'coming like a sailor in his first whore ashore after a six-month cruise.' Uh, the captain's words, sir."

Donelson jumped out of the vehicle and upright, smiling all over his face. "Excellent, Medwick, that's really just excellent."

Misericordia was by his side, grinning like a girl who's found a Shetland pony with a red ribbon tied around it beneath her Christmas tree. "Is it? Is it him? Is it? Is it?"

"We can't know for certain yet, little lady," Donelson said, sounding and feeling positively avuncular. "But right *here*—" He pressed stiffened fingers to his side in the vicinity of his appendix. "—tells me that's affirmative."

Misericordia crouched in the open side hatch of the verti, feeling the wind slapping her face and plucking at her tightly braided hair. As a concession to Kirtland AFB's all-male fighting force she had clothes on: an OD halter top and brief khaki shorts. No shoes, though; she had her limits. She felt overdressed, practically in bondage.

In addition to the clothing she wore a sort of cross-your-heart web harness with grenades hanging off it in front and a pair of *wakizashi*, Japanese short swords, crossed over her back. She had a Beretta caseless 10mm on a belt in back, its holstered barrel sticking down between the cheeks of her rump. She looked as if she'd stepped off the sleeve of an old Sybil Danning Adventure Video, except Sybil was blond and a lot more, you know, *profound*.

The verti swept low, following Eubank north, paralleling the route the invasion force had taken that morning. The advance was stalled now, in part because of the drive in force against its flank, but its progress had been good enough to please even Colonel Donelson.

The airframe vibrated to the firing of the chin-mounted 25mm gun. A few shots thunked into the fuselage from below. Misericordia glanced back at Dr. James, who was sitting holding onto a fold-down seat with both hands and looking paler than usual and grinned.

"Don't worry about getting your balls shot off, Doctor; the seats are armored. Not that you've been *using* your balls for much."

"Impertinence. I won't hear it."

She ran her tongue deliberately around her lips.

"We're approaching the drop zone," the pilot's voice said over the intercom.

"Got it," Misericordia said back. She looped the long Israeli-style sling of a Heckler & Koch MP15 around her neck and stood up to check the way the flat blue nylon polymer was attached to the D-ring overhead. She snapped a carabiner on the line, held it with her left hand, the pistol grip of her submachine gun in the right.

The scream of the props outside changed pitch as the high-mounted wing rotated upward. The craft veered clockwise, breaking away from the commerce strips lining Eubank to fly over blocks of flat-roofed stucco homes. It skimmed the tops of trees whose lushness, fed by mineral-rich volcanic ash and watered by volcano-engendered storms, lent a deceptive appearance of normalcy to the neighborhood.

The verti slowed to a hover. A rattle of automatic fire struck the far side of the fuselage but failed to penetrate the Kevlar that lined the inside of the compartment.

"I wish you would leave those ridiculous swords behind," Dr. James said. "They'll only get in your way."

She stuck her tongue out at him. "I need to have *some* fun." She glanced at the audio-visual pickups set in the forward bulkhead. "I'm going out now." She kicked the coiled line out the hatch and slid smoothly down ten meters to the ground.

She was in a backyard, green grass yielding and cool underfoot and around her ankles. The yards here were neatly sectioned off one from another by cinderblock walls, mostly intact, most a bit over a meter and a half tall. They cut down visibility between houses. All the same a snarl of full-auto fire greeted her touchdown. Bullets splashed off the front of a red brick barbecue grill.

She fired a shot. A gunman with shaggy gray hair dropped his assault rifle and fell half in and half out of the blown-out sliding door of a house two houses away.

She ducked below the level of the walls. Crouching, she made her way to the side of the house. A fresh wave of firing broke out not two hundred meters east.

Out on the broad boulevard a grenade cracked, its sound reverberating briefly between the buildings that faced Juan Tabo to either side. Misericordia hunkered among waist-high weeds inside the chainlink fence that marked a house's rear property line. Beyond was a parking lot, empty except for a dumpster—rotting papers, decomposing biodegradable polymers, and a cat that had been dead for about six months, her nose told her—and the back of some kind of derelict store.

There were men in the store. She could hear them, their small weight-shifting noises, their stifled coughs, their open-mouthed, fear-containing breathing. She could smell their bodies, the soap they'd washed their clothes in, the toothpaste they'd brushed with that morning. The lubricants of their firearms, hot from recent heavy firing.

She eeled through the gap between the metal endpost of the chainlink fence and the wall of the neighboring yard, slipped down a half-meter slope and over the low cinderblock retaining wall onto the cracked asphalt of the parking lot. She walked forward.

Men came out of the back of the store and pointed guns at her. She stopped, looked at them fearfully, and raised her hands over her head.

"Check this out, Captain," the redbearded man said. "Caught her snooping around out back of Zollweg's Music Emporium."

Standing with a pair of skinny Crip followers and a small strip mall between him and the free-fire zone that was Juan Tabo, Rob Honesty studied the captive closely. He grinned beneath his rakish military moustache.

"I wish everything you brought me looked this good, Westlake," he said.

Westlake's partner, a tall man with black shock hair and sleepy eyes, held up the MP15 on its sling and the X-shaped harness with the *wakizashi* in their scabbards. "She was loaded for bear."

"Whoa," Honesty said. "What does a cute little girl like you want with a lot of nasty hardware like that?"

"Where's Donovan Steele?" the captive asked.

Honesty frowned. "Steele? The cyborg, huh? He's not here. I don't even know that he's coming. How come you know about Donovan Steele, anyway?"

He took a step forward, reaching for her chin. "Hey, don't look so disappointed. I never met the man myself, but if you're that dead set on getting his autograph, maybe I can work something out—"

She raised her eyes to his and smiled.

She caught his outstretched wrists and spun, reeling him into her and then whipping him past in an *aikido* grip, snapping him right up into Westlake's face.

The two men went down in a flail of arms and legs. Misericordia stepped up to the tall skinny man who held her gear, whipped her short swords from their scabbards while he was still gaping, frozen by her sudden outburst of furious activity. She slashed across. His head popped off his shoulders on a geyser of blood.

His eyes weren't sleepy anymore.

She turned to the two Crips. They were both kids, no more than sixteen tops, a boy and a girl. To her that was only an indication of their likely speed, strength, and approach to fighting—fast, little, and wild, respectively.

To Misericordia they were no more than prey.

The girl was bringing her Brazilian assault rifle to firing position; the boy had had to grab for his piece, which he'd left leaning against a wall. After fumbling briefly he gave up and took it by the flash suppressor with both hands and swung it like a bat.

She stepped into him, swung up her right-hand sword, and caught the butt of the bullpup rifle with a clack of metal on plastic. She began to pivot right, into him, slashing through his face with a left-hand cut.

At the same instant her gliding right foot left the ground, sweeping up and back in a reverse roundhouse kick. As the Crip's blood sprayed her face and the left side of her blouse, she looked over her right shoulder for terminal guidance. She kicked the assault rifle spinning from the girl's hands.

The Crip girl was wide open. Misericordia came around, slide-stepped up to her, punched the right-hand *wakizashi* through her sternum.

Misericordia said, "Pretty," kissed the girl on the lips. She came away with blood on her mouth.

A sound behind her made her turn, whirling the dying girl like a dancing partner. The young black man was up on one knee bringing his sidearm to bear on her. He was really very pretty too. She felt tears threaten at the thought that she was not going to find the man of her destiny, her dreams, in this force attacking the Kirtland flank. She was going to have to make do with this pretty black man with the nice eyes and flashing grin.

She threw the girl at him. Literally *threw*; the youthful Crip slid off the watered steel of the blade and went flying toward him through the air. His eyes went wide in astonishment. He wasn't sure *he* could toss a person around like that, even one that slight.

He was good, though. He threw himself sideways to avoid the rag-doll sprawl of dead adolescent limbs, tucked his shoulder, rolled onto his back.

He brought his sidearm up and shot Misericordia through the belly.

9

It wasn't a good hit. It struck on the level of her navel and well to the left. She staggered back with a cry. She dropped her left-hand sword to clutch at herself. The pain was more intense than anything she had ever known. It made the world swim before her eyes.

Slowly Rob Honesty got to his feet, keeping his handgun trained on her the while. When he was up he assumed a classic Weaver combat stance: feet apart, hips open away from his target, right arm locked, left hand cupping right, elbow bent to stabilize the triangle of arms and body.

Beside him, Westlake picked his own way up, brushing bits of gravel from his butt and back. He licked at a trickle of blood from his right nostril that clashed horribly with his orangish moustache. Honesty had caught him with an inadvertent back-fist when Misericordia had flipped him into the man.

"All right, lady, that's enough. Whoever you are you're pretty damned good. Just throw those toys down."

Misericordia looked at him. Her blue eyes were almost slate gray with agony, and her hand was pressed to the entry wound, blood spilling over the fingers. She dropped the other sword.

Then she straightened. And smiled. And threw herself into a forward cartwheel.

They did it all the time in ninja videos, which Miseri played for herself by the hour in the guts of Pajarito Plateau. As second-dan *karateka* Rob Honesty knew, they *didn't* do it in real life, not if they wanted to live long and prosper. It was an acrobatic stunt, not a fighting technique. *If you were human* . . .

It froze him like a jacklighted deer. Long braid flying, the woman whipped through two revolutions, popped up in his face. With an earshattering *kiai* she lashed an open-fist slap with her right hand and sent Honesty's sidearm flying into some trash piled in the angle of a wall.

She threw a left-hand punch at his sternum, with her strength a killing blow. His right forearm snapped up and out in a circle block, deflected the blow. She opened her eyes wide in pleased surprise. Behind her she sensed Westlake making a move. She gave the lovely black man a straight thrust-kick—a true nut-pulper if he wasn't good enough to pivot and get his left hip in the way. He did, and was sent flying back, bruised but still in the fight.

Miseri was going to enjoy this. The pain in her gut had already receded to background noise.

A heavy hand fell on her left shoulder, hauled her around. She went with it, allowing Westlake's male upper-body strength—rather less than hers, as it happened—to donate momentum. With a horrible raptor scream, she fired a straight vertical fist right between his eyes.

For a moment they stood that way, frozen. Westlake's sky-blue eyes took on a porcelain glaze. Misericordia pulled her hand back.

Westlake's forehead had been caved in as if by a maul. He collapsed, a sack of lifeless protoplasm.

Misericordia whipped about into a fighting stance, left foot advanced. Her hands hung limp at the ends of her upraised forearms. They kept up a small, random motion.

Honesty was in a similar stance, but his hands were raised blades. He did a take at Westlake, shook his head, spat out dust.

"What *are* you?"

"Something new," she said. "Something wonderful." She began to circle.

"You're a cyborg. Just like Steele. That's why you're so strong. That's why the gutshot didn't hurt you."

She laughed out loud, a sound like silver coins ringing on a counter. The flow of blood from her belly wound had slowed almost to a stop.

"Oh, it hurts, babe. Just not for long—it's healing right now. And I'm not like Steele, sweetheart. I'm *better*."

The man flipped a high kick toward her face—a feint, designed to make her flinch, and suicide had he been close enough actually to connect, given the rattlesnake speed she'd displayed. She held her ground, smiling tightly around the pain in her belly.

He charged. A stutter step, low kick for the knee—another feint, gambit declined, punches rocketing toward her face left-right-left, blocked with laughing grace; a pivot, side-thrust kick to drive her back and gain *ma'ā*, combat separation.

He's good, Misericordia thought sadly, *but he's only human*. It was time to end this, before more of his troops showed up.

Like a wisp of smoke she evaded the side kick. Swooping low she caught his heel, raised it to armpit level. His masculine thrusting betrayed him then, making it easy for her to turn away and tuck his leg at full extension beneath her left arm— not that it would have been hard even had he resisted. She was as much stronger than he as he was than a five-year-old girl-child. That was the problem.

"Don't think it hasn't been fun, doll," she told him. He screamed as she torqued her hips and dislocated his leg at the hip.

She let him drop. He tried to scramble up, but sheer will would not hold him erect with his left leg flopping like a rag doll's. He went down hard, grunting in pain as the loose bone end scraped his pelvis. He began to drag himself away, determined whatever he did not to simply give in; that wasn't in him.

She followed at a supple walk. "Wh-what *are* you?" he gasped. "A monster?"

"You're getting warmer. I'm not human. I'm more—the genetically engineered optimization of the human form. All that humans can be, I am. *Homo successor:* I am that to come, I am that which will be."

Her beautiful face darkened. "But those who come after me will not be my flesh, my blood. I'm barren, you see."

She knelt. He struck at her with a fighting knife. Laughing, she dodged, and like a mongoose taking a cobra, grabbed his hand and plucked the knife from it. She studied the weapon for a moment, bent its eight-inch alloy blade almost double with a flick of her slim wrists, tossed it aside.

She grabbed his head in both hands, pressed her lips to his. Then she broke his neck with a precise twist that snapped the vertebra but left the spinal cord uncompromised.

With mother's care she laid his head back on the hard-packed gravelly ground. "If whoever finds you has the sense to immobilize your head properly, you'll not only live, you won't be paralyzed."

She kissed his forehead, which was beaded with sweat. "You weren't good enough to beat me, babe—no one born of woman is. But you were good enough to win your life."

Quickly but not hurriedly she recovered her equipment, shrugged back into her harness. Around to the front of the building the firefight was heating up again; the 223rd was counterattacking. As she was replacing her swords in their sheaths a fire team came around the corner, three men supporting a fourth with a blood-soaked leg.

She killed them, firing single shots from the hip so fast they sounded like full-auto. She was tired of sport; her genetically tailored immune system was working overtime on damage control. The suppressed 10mm was very quiet.

She checked to make sure the flare gun that would summon the verti was still on the harness. She had absolutely refused to wear a communicator; she could not tolerate having even Dr. James, her creator, her unconsummated love, looking over her shoulder when she worked. And the very thought of that horrid chicken-necked colonel alternately barking orders and interrogations at her made her skin crawl.

He thinks he's so clever. He thinks when he's done with us he'll kill the doctor and possess me. She laughed at the absurdity of the thought.

A launched grenade exploded inside the building. She heard feet running across Juan Tabo, a gasp of pain and the thud of a body falling on the cement median. She turned and lithely ran.

It was an open-topped *pulga*, bug—what the late twentieth century knew as a Volkswagen Beetle. They had not been manufactured in the memory of anyone alive—except in Mexico. They were perfect Third World cars, small, cheap, mechanically simple, a breeze to maintain. Most important of all, they were *cute*. The Mexicans loved them, and apparently intended to keep making them forever.

It had taken war and disaster to bring down the trade barriers the lords of Detroit—union and management—had erected around America in the late twentieth century. Now a predominance of the cars that actually ran in Albuquerque were MexiBeetles.

Donovan Steele was stopped for a traffic light at Menaul and Louisiana. Traffic flowed by, mostly on foot or bicycle, people glancing without much interest at the white plastic safe-conduct placard pinned to the windshield by a wiper blade. Rob Honesty—at this moment leading a desperate flank attack on the Kirtland penetration, the thump and clatter of which could be plainly heard—had given several of them to the Enclave to ensure passage through Maynet's turf without official hassle.

It did not ensure speedy passage through the crowds going to and from Coronado Center, a sprawling shopping mall, many of whose shops and restaurants seemed to be open for business. The passersby seemed as unaware of the battle raging just a few klicks away as they did of the volcanoes drooling gray smut into the air across the river.

He hadn't really run into the phenomenon in Strike Force; Manhattan's no-man's-land was an urban desert not really capable of supporting everyday life. But he'd run into it in the Keys: the infinite capacity of humanity to adjust, to go about their business even in the valley of the shadow of death. They kept clear of firefights in progress, cycled around the shell holes, and if Grandma got her cranium evacuated by a stray round, that was sad, but it was also life. From the upper atmosphere to the Venus-like mouths of undersea volcanic vents, life flowed in, persevered, went on. Human life was no exception.

Quivering with impatience, Jilly was up on her knees on the passenger seat, looking this way and that as if seeking an alternate ford across the flood of humanity. A plastic eyeshade turned her nose and eyes to a green bandit mask.

She grabbed Steele's arm. "Look!"

Off to the southeast a verti leapt into view above the treetops. It moved north, wings rotating horizontal as it picked up speed. It banked toward them.

From somewhere south of it a missile sprinted in pursuit, spinning a thread of white smoke across the sky. The verti accelerated. It couldn't hope to outrun the missile, but suddenly the air to either side of it was alive with eye-stinging flecks of light. They were parachute flares popped out of pods on the fuselage to confuse the missile's heat-seeking guidance system.

Apparently whoever picked the flares was smarter than the AI routines intended to keep the missile from chasing dummies. It went after one of the floating sparks, plunged through and down to its death against the second story of an office building.

The verti circled to within a kilometer of where Steele and Jilly sat. "Can't you shoot it down?" she asked.

He shook his head. "Too far. He could dodge an M-91 at this range, and a rifle bullet wouldn't penetrate."

He tapped his knuckles on the steering wheel. It was an after-market upgrade, real wood. "I wish I could knock it down. I just have this feeling. . . ."

Behind him a horn honked, and a driver stuck his head out the window of his panel truck to scream abuse. But it was too late. The light had already turned red again.

10

By the time Steele and Jilly arrived in the Far Heights battle zone, the fighting had died down to the occasional sniper's shot. Gordon Walls was surprised that Steele hadn't come—he still knew his visitor as Peter Murphy—but he could not have cared less at this point. He was exhilarated, bubbling over with his belief that the inexorable tide of the Kirtland advance had been turned by the valor of his men and, of course, his inspired leadership. Jilly made jackoff gestures behind his back.

Steele agreed. The base troops had in fact made good gains against stiff opposition under the excellent cover and concealment of urban terrain. The assault had probably gained its objectives—or maybe not; Donelson seemed very much a man to overestimate his capabilities. Most likely the base troops were simply exhausted, and running too low on ammo to grab further ground—the number of bullets that got launched in a serious firefight was ridiculously easy to *under*estimate.

For their part the Far Heights defenders were unwilling to launch any counterthrusts of their own, though if Steele and his little friend wanted to mount a two-person offensive they were welcome to. Steele couldn't blame them. They were tired, scared, hurt, and low on resupply themselves.

Some of Walls's lieutenants seemed honestly pissed off that Steele wasn't on hand to charge the invaders with an M-27 blazing in either fist. Steele kept quiet; awesome killing machine though he was, he had no illusions that he had a big red "S" on his chest. Every squad in the invading force had at least one portable weapon that could blow him to pieces, nysteel skeleton or no. He was meant to be the ultimate in smart weapons. Getting blasted to pieces in a completely futile charge wasn't smart.

He did agree to spend the night in the Far Heights. If the base attack resumed, he'd help defend. If diStefano's forces mounted a credible counterattack of some sort—possibly with help from their allies, which had been conspicuously absent except for the savage but abortive flank thrust out of Maynet's Near Heights—he would gladly take part in that.

It wasn't much. But it was all he had to offer.

At 0130 he was shaken awake on his cot in the derelict motel Walls was using as a forward command post. While he didn't much need it physically, he was programmed to be able to sleep—and dream—as a means of relieving accumulated mental stresses and preserving his sanity. It had been a conspicuously mixed success.

Engine noises were reported from the entire salient the base had hammered into the Far Heights. An attack was expected at any minute.

He and Jilly arrived at the front line to be met by a jubilant Walls. "We've won!" he said. "Can you hear it? They're pulling out. The fuckers are *running*."

Jilly looked at Steele. "The Enclave!" she exclaimed.

"So," Janet Virág asked, "did you save many lives up in the Far Heights?"

Steele grimaced. He and Jilly stood with the Enclave security boss behind a two-meter sandbag-reinforced cinderblock wall that had been thrown up after Eruption in the parking lot of a day-care center on the northwest corner of Lomas and Girard.

"At least we made an *effort* to honor our commitment to help the people in the Far Heights," Jilly said pointedly.

Virág skinned her lips back from her teeth. "Too bad all the action was here, huh?"

The base's attack had hit hard. Peering through the make-shift periscope, Steele saw four Marauder armored cars still smoldering in and around the intersection. There were bodies out there too, and with the sun starting in early and hard they were already beginning to smell by ten in the morning.

"You did warn us," Virág said. "Not that we really needed it." Ever-suspicious, Virág had had her defense forces on about eighty-percent alert to begin with. She had half-expected Donelson to pull a trick like this.

"We lost three kids killed, eight injured; one of 'em's in Ngoya's vats, and they're all gonna make it."

She shook her head. "It's been a long time since a light-armor attack on a prepared position was that good an idea. We had our M-91s, and it never seemed to occur to Colonel D that, as bad as the streets in this town are, we mighta planted some mines out on the road and patched 'em over with asphalt. They got a bigger body count than you can see, by the way. When we started popping rockets and launching grenades in on them and firing off the Claymores we'd set out by the side of the road, a bunch of soldiers de-assed their trucks and hid out in the middle school and the houses on the other side of Lomas. Too bad we booby trapped 'em all, huh?"

Steele straightened. "Can you hold them?"

"Not a chance. They could take us—could have had us now, if Donelson wanted us bad enough. But we'd lay some almighty hurt on him. Enough to give the Council pukes a shot at taking him out—maybe even one of them by his lonesome."

"What's he waiting for then?" Jilly asked. Her tone wasn't as sharp as before. She perceived the tall, striking Virág as a rival, and she had rallied reflexively to the defensive when the security chief aimed sarcasm at Steele. But she had good command over herself. Steele approved of that.

"He's waiting for us to give up, kid. You should hear Paskoy and Houska screaming about how we have to ask for terms." She laughed. "They're also pretty hot about the booby traps. What if, like, homeless people tried to squat in the mid-school?"

"That reminds me of something," Steele said. "Just what's the connection between Houska and Jeff Tillman? I don't usually associate violent jocks like Tillman and his friends with professional bleeding hearts."

"Jeffy and his pals had a few run-ins with Dr. Singh, right after Eruption," Virág said. "In the old days they had things pretty much their way—football stars can do no wrong. Took 'em a while to adjust to the new facts of life, one of them being that Dr. Singh didn't give diddly what kind of letters they wore on their jackets, they still had to abide by the law. His law."

She shrugged. "Houska spends a lot of time farting around with his crafts stuff, but he's still big into counseling here on campus. He thinks Dr. Singh's too authoritarian. And basically Jeff is one of your fine young sociopaths, and he pulled the wool over old Paul's big blue eyes, and now Houska and Paskoy and the rest of them think Tillman and his pals are really good boys. Just misunderstood."

Steele raised his eyebrows. "What?" Virág said. "You surprised the Gypsy bitch knows big words like 'sociopath'?"

"No. I'm surprised you haven't had more trouble with Tillman."

"Jeffy's sociopathic, not stupid. He knows if he *really* blows across the line I'll let some air in between his ears and then tell Houska society made me do it."

"You're going to have trouble with him."

"You ex-cops all have a nasty turn of mind. That's the trouble with you." She grinned. "Besides, with any luck we'll all be dead by then, so why worry about it?"

"I want Steele," Misericordia said with a whine in her voice.

Dr. James sat in the waiting room of Colonel Donelson's office reading an old number of a Security Police newsletter with a smile of amused disdain. As always he wore white.

"You can't have him," he said without looking up. The magazine cover showed an old file photo of a mushroom cloud, and the words, "Man-Portable Fusion Rockets: Taking a Bite Out of Inner-City Crime." "Not unless he chooses to cooperate."

He laid the magazine down on his thighs. "Whatever is delaying that fool Donelson? First he abandons a successful attack to follow his own scheme, which he was explicitly ordered not to do, and now he says he urgently has to meet with us in his office, and has the audacity to keep us waiting. The man's a jackass."

Misericordia sat on the edge of the receptionist's untended desk. "He has this waiting room bugged, you know."

"What difference does it make whether he knows I think he's a fool or not? If he's unaware of it at this late date, he's a bigger fool than I imagined."

He resumed reading. Miseri kicked her feet. She wore a lightweight jogging outfit of middy-top and loose shorts, shiny black trimmed with silver. The entry wound Rob Honesty's 10mm bullet had given her yesterday was faded to a dime-sized white patch, as was the exit wound in her back.

"I want a child," she said.

Dr. James lowered the magazine again. "You want *what?*"

"I want a child. I want to be a mother."

"What a ridiculous idea. You were made to destroy, my child. Not to nurture."

"But normal human women can bear children. I'm supposed to be the ultimate woman, right? How can I be the ultimate, when regular people can do something I can't?"

"I've told you dozens of times: you are infertile. Child bearing is completely extraneous to what you were created to do. I'm tired of your whining on this subject, Misericordia. Drop it, *now.*"

She stood up. "Or what? You'll whip me?" She licked her lips and ran a hand down her side. "That would be nice. Or better yet, brand my ass with a hot iron for being such a bad girl. It'll heal. Anything to show you care."

His nostrils pinched in disgust, and he turned his face away.

Footsteps on the gravel outside. Misericordia lounged back against the desk. The door opened, letting in a blast of morning daylight and a 223rd SSG lieutenant in a blue beret.

"Dr. James. Ms. Misericordia," he said with a nod and a smile. "The Colonel sends his regrets for the delay, but something's come up. He wants you, right away."

"*Where* does he want us? He asked us to meet him here."

"I know, and I'm real sorry. But some of our people are still holding our salient up in the Far Heights. The colonel wants us to take you there immediately in his verti."

Dr. James stood and held out his hand. Miseri handed him his white Panama hat from the desk. "Very well, young man. But I'm warning you: this had better not be a wild-goose chase."

General Whiteman tried to look stern. His round, soft face wasn't up to it.

"Now, let's get something straight," he said. His voice was warm, rich, and sincere, more suitable for selling life insurance or hosting afternoon talk shows than delivering reprimands. "You were ordered to undertake an attack on the Far Heights. Is that correct?"

All but quivering at attention, Colonel George Donelson answered, "Yes, sir."

Whiteman nodded. "And yet, this morning, in violation of my clear orders, you attacked the University of New Mexico Enclave. Is this right?"

"Yes, sir."

Whiteman stared down at his immaculately manicured hands, spread wide on the surface of his genuine hardwood desk. Then he looked up, and in help-me-with-this tones said, "Can you offer any explanation for why you have disregarded my orders?"

"Yes, *sir*. I have not disregarded your orders, *sir*."

Whiteman stared at him thunderstruck. After what he judged a decent interval, Donelson plowed on. He was a full colonel, after all. And he was a fighting man, not some . . . cello player.

"As instructed, I undertook an assault into the Far Heights. It succeeded in achieving deep penetration of Councilor diStefano's territory and inflicting heavy casualties upon his defense forces. Having effectively removed diStefano from the picture, I then perceived an excellent opportunity to launch an attack along interior lines and strike another enemy unexpectedly. Acting under my own initiative, and in accordance with the recognized historical principles of warfare, I seized that opportunity. *Sir*."

Whiteman opened his mouth, wet his lips, shut his mouth, and blinked. "I see," he said at length. "So you, ah. You weren't disobeying orders at all, were you?" He seemed pleased. General Whiteman abhorred confrontations.

"No, sir. May I go now, sir?"

"Yes, Colonel, that will be—no, wait. Now that I think about it. Dr. James was very exercised when he learned of the sudden change in your attack's direction. I wonder if you would explain to him what really is going on? We really are supposed to be working together on this."

A tic of Donelson's mouth twitched his ginger-colored moustache. "He and his, ah, assistant returned to Los Alamos not long ago, sir. Urgent business called them back to the labs."

Whiteman made a mouth. "I'm sorry to hear that. Ms. Misericordia was really very charming. What on earth could have made Dr. James leave without stopping in to say good-bye?"

11

"Young man," Dr. James said, craning his head to peer out the verti's window, "we've gone too far. We are clearly over the desert well north even of Councilor diStefano's stronghold, not to mention the farthest advance of your troops yesterday. What's the meaning of this?"

The lieutenant in the beret looked at the six men in camouflage SP battle dress sitting in seats folded down from the aircraft's cabin walls. As one they picked up their stubby assault rifles and aimed them at the doctor and Misericordia, who sat beside him playing cat's cradle with fishing line taken from a survival kit.

"Well, Doctor," the lieutenant said, tilting his head back insolently, "I guess we *have* gone too far. But I'm afraid you two aren't going any farther." He rolled his eyes meaningfully back at the window behind him. "At least, not *horizontally*, if you get my drift."

Misericordia's eyes went wide. "You've been ordered to kill us?"

The Security Policemen looked at each other and laughed.

She stood up. Safeties clattered off. She pulled her middy top off over her head, threw it aside. She wore nothing beneath. Her small breasts bounced slightly. Her pink nipples stood erect.

With a graceful motion she bent, skinned her shorts down her slender legs and stepped out of them to stand stark naked before the astonished soldiers. She smiled. "That doesn't mean we can't be *friends*."

Even with shocking bright splashes of blood disfiguring his white linen suit, Dr. James looked dignified. He made it a point to.

Misericordia stuck her head through the bulkhead that separated the passenger compartment from the cockpit. Her pale naked body was covered with a scarlet net body stocking of blood, like an ancient Hammer Films heroine.

"The pilot says he'll take us anywhere we want to go. He's being *very, very* nice, after I pulled his copilot's fingers off and made him eat them. Shall I have him take us back?"

"By no means. Have him fly us back to Los Alamos at once."

She pouted. "What about Steele?"

"You saw what that moron Donelson believed sufficient to dispose of us." He gestured around at the bodies of the lieutenant and his six men, strewn around the cabin in postures of violent death. "Do you imagine there's any danger of *him* capturing Donovan Steele?"

Misericordia laughed, ducked back briefly into the cockpit. When she came out she went back, grabbed the lieutenant by the front of his blood-soaked blouse, dragged him to a sitting position. His dead eyes stared past her. A bit of purplish organ stuck out one corner of his mouth.

Miseri crossed his hands over his chest. Then she took him by the wrist, moved it up and down and laughed to see the hand wave.

She had him exchange high fives with one of his late subordinates whose head was turned around backward on his neck. Then she rummaged through his pockets, found a pocket knife with a folding fork on it, extended the fork and put the tool in his hand.

"See?" she said, raising dead hand and fork to the lieutenant's blue lips. "He's eating. I bet you never saw a dead man eat before. That reminds me, I'm getting pretty hungry now."

"For God's sake," Dr. James said. "Stop playing with that trash. Get those bodies out of here. The smell is beginning to revolt me."

"Imagine," Miguel "Mike" Aragon said to Mr. Skin in a confidential tone. "In the middle of all this tragedy and crisis, the Albuquerque Slasher has struck again." He shook his head and clucked.

"At least he kept off our turf this time," Mr. Skin said sourly. He wore his desert fatigues today, as befit a council of war. His fashion sense had required him to wear a gold-lamé band around his hairless head, however, and to heavily outline his eyes in kohl. Appearance is a hard taskmaster.

It was an open air meeting today in the Civic Plaza, just west of the crackerbox loom of the Convention Center. The sky was filmed with a high, thin white overcast. The sound of 82mm mortars working over the Enclave whoomped and thudded like giants playing soccer. The Crips, of course, were out in force. They had been skirmishing heavily with the base on cross-Broadway forays, and had taken to painting their faces and wearing feathers. They all looked as if they were trying out to be extras in a remake of *Apocalypse Now*, and also as if they were having the time of their young lives.

"Here comes poor Ross, now," Aragon said. "He must feel terrible: his neighbor is invaded, the commander of his defense forces is mutilated by some sort of awful mutant woman, and to top it off another unfortunate young woman is murdered in a horrible way almost in his backyard. It's a reflection on this violent, materialistic society in which we live."

"Another Treasure Box dancer?" Mr. Skin asked. Aragon nodded. "Which one?"

"Sadie," Dameron Crowe said. Mr. Skin closed his eyes in pain.

All the rules weren't in abeyance for the duration; the Crips were only letting each Council member bring a pair of guards, unarmed. Ross Maynet's pair kept darting glances left and right from their haunted, sunken eyes. Their commander was lying in an Enclave hospital bed with his head packed between sandbags, under sedation so he could rest instead of babbling compulsively about his run-in with Colonel Donelson's secret weapon.

Maynet himself, however, looked very sleek in his cammies, which were pressed to razor creases. Miguel "Mike" thought, in fact, he looked more chipper than he had in some time. Adversity obviously agreed with the man. Maybe Aragon misjudged him.

"Ross," he called, and nodded and waved.

Maynet waved a hand distractedly, dodged away. He bent briefly over a dark object on the sidewalk, picked something up and put a hand to his mouth. He walked quickly by then, his jaws working. The muscles at the hinges of his jaws were enormously developed, as if he spent a lot of time grinding his teeth.

"Ross?" Aragon said tentatively. "Ross—wait! What on earth are you *eating?*"

Maynet hurried on without acknowledging his fellow Councilor. His curiosity unbearably stimulated, Aragon walked toward the remnants of the dark object, craning his neck.

He gasped.

The soft pock-pock-shuffle of Dameron Crowe pulling himself along on his metal crutches sounded behind him. "Come on, boss. Time for the cockamamie council of war. We better get this over with so's we can get back to trying to do something constructive."

Aragon gagged. "But that's—that's—"

Crowe nodded his huge misshapen head. "Dogshit. Yeah. So, are you coming, or what?"

"I'm sorry, Dr. Singh," Miguel Aragon said from the screen. His lower lip was moist beneath his moustache. "We are absolutely unable to tender you any assistance at this juncture."

The subway rumble of another mortar barrage slamming into one of the dorms vibrated up through the floor of Singh's office in the Med Center. The neurosurgeon sat staring at the telephone screen, immobile as a carven idol.

"You made a pact with us for mutual defense," Steele said. He was acting as Dr. Singh's military adviser while the doctor made the telephone rounds of his putative allies. Virág was out on the wire watching for yet another probe at the perimeter. "We're invoking it."

"Circumstances, ah, circumstances beyond our control prevent us from honoring it at this point in time. Really, we'll help you as soon as we can. But we're all feeling the heat from Colonel Donelson's aggression."

He licked his lips, and a slyly sullen look came onto his pudgy face. "Honestly, Mr. Murphy, I'm surprised to hear you take such a moralistic tone. Where was the Enclave when Donelson invaded the Far Heights? As I understand it, the Enclave's entire response was to send you and that young Romero woman, much too late to be of any assistance. As if two ordinary people could *be* much help."

"Mr. Aragon, please," Dr. Singh said. "I beg you." Steele looked at him sharply; the dark face showed no flicker of emotion. "Lt. Steele is a mighty warrior, but even he cannot defeat an entire army. Without outside aid, we have no chance of withstanding the base forces."

Aragon let just a second of gloating dance across his fat face. Steele ached to smash it in for him.

"You seem selfishly determined to keep Lt. Donovan Steele's services for yourselves, Doctor. There's no place for selfishness in the gentle, caring world of today. Perhaps it's only a just reward for your greed, that he is all you have."

Colonel George Donelson stuck his head out the back of his command vehicle, which was parked beside an antique artillery piece in a park a few hundred meters east of the Enclave's Girard perimeter. "What is it, son? I'm a busy man. Time waits for no man."

The lieutenant who had called him forth quailed a little; backlit by the red instrument glow the Colonel had a wild, almost demoniacal look, and his thin sandy hair glowed like fire. With luck, blackout paint and the sweep of his coalscuttle helmet hid any flicker of expression.

"Sorry to bother you, sir. But we caught these two coming over the wire."

He nodded. His men pushed a pair of men forward. Boys, rather—big husky boys, jocks complete with tattered letter jackets.

"Coming *out* of the Enclave?" Donelson took out his pipe and began to stoke it. "Interesting. All right, you two—what's your story?"

The taller of the two threw his chest out. "My name's Jeff Tillman, sir, and this is my friend Keith Tauber. We came out to do our duty. We want to offer our services to you and to the armed forces of the United States of America, sir."

Donelson lit his pipe. He seemed suddenly relaxed, almost jovial. "Is that a fact?"

The shorter boy nodded his head vigorously, making white-blond hair bob around his burly shoulders. "We'll do anything we can to help you, sir. We just want to make a *difference*."

Donelson laughed a cloud of smoke. "That you shall, son," he murmured. "That you shall."

"M-mister Steele?"

Donovan Steele rolled over on his cot. The flesh-colored polyceram cap that covered the muzzle of the pistol built into his right arm retracted. It was a matter of reflex.

"What is it?" He brought up a time display in his field of vision: 0343. He sat up rubbing his eyes. They got gooey with sleep these days, something they hadn't done when what surrounded them was a polymer pseudoskin.

The two kids in security armbands exchanged nervous glances. "Do you, do you, uh, *know* this man?" the boy asked.

The girl had an OD rag tied around her head and a shock of straw-colored hair falling over it. "He just walked right up to the gate and asked for you," she said. "We, uh, we figured if he wanted to try any funny stuff, you could, like, handle it."

"Thanks for the confidence," Steele said, wondering what the hell was going on.

There was a thumping and a dragging noise on the dusty floorboards of the ancient brick house between the Med Center and the eastern perimeter.

"Christ, what's the use blowing megabucks of the taxpayers' money on a cyborg if he has to fuckin' sleep on duty?" Twisting his skinny body, Dameron Crowe shoved between the two youngsters. As always he was dressed like a chimp in an ancient sideshow: plaid sports coat, green corduroy pants, brown and white Oxford shoes. "Rise and shine, Sleeping Beauty, there's dirty deeds to be done, or our lives are gonna be done dirt cheap."

"What are you talking about?"

"You know all those prisoners I had your kids bring me?"

Steele nodded. He didn't like to think about the fate of those prisoners. He didn't waste that much compassion on Donelson's baby killers, but he somehow didn't think Dameron Crowe's interrogation techniques would be very *nice*.

"I got one to tell me a little story. A *swell* story. And it gave me an idea."

"What kind of idea?"

"A sneaky one."

Steele rubbed the back of his neck. That was a disadvantage to having real flesh-and-blood muscles overlaid on the woven-nysteel cables that gave him his real strength: they got sore.

"I thought your boss Aragon didn't want to help us, Crowe."

"He doesn't. But he didn't specifically order me *not* to help you; he just said I couldn't send any troops. Meanwhile it's my job to keep his fat butt safe, and if Donelson takes you down, Mikey's not gonna have to wait any too damn long for his turn in the frying pan. So here I am."

Steele looked at him. "Crowe, I believe you are the snakiest son of a bitch I've ever met in my life."

Crowe grinned. "You bet your life, buddy boy. And you sure as fuck *are*. Betting your life, that is."

12

Dawn was just becoming more than a possibly false promise when the bass whine of a powerful engine and the sliding clatter of treads on pavement blasted the exhausted defenders of the Girard gate out of their stupor. They sent out a desperate call for help and prepped their M-91s with fumbling fingers, fearing the worst: that Donelson had somehow got his hands on an M-12 Waldrop main battle tank, its bulky combination of spaced, foamed, and polyceram-mesh armor capable of shrugging off repeated volleys from their throwaway AT rockets.

"Where's Don?" Jilly Romero asked in alarm as she trotted from Virág's command post just behind the lines. She was trying to dab the sleep from her eyes with one hand and clutching an assault rifle in the other.

"How the hell should I know?" The Gypsy woman was walking beside her with ground-eating strides of her long legs, shrugging on a vest of woven polyceram fibers with nysteel inserts. She dropped into position behind the sandbag and cement rampart and said, "What the fuck, over?"

A sheet of shimmery blackness, four meters by four, gently curved left to right, materialized with stage-magic abruptness out of the unusual morning mist that swirled between the houses fronting broad Lomas Boulevard. It advanced at a walking pace toward the perimeter, accompanied by the sounds of a heavy tracked vehicle.

Gunfire cracked from the Enclave lines. Bullets bounced from the black sheet. "Cease fire!" Virág shouted, waving her arms. "Don't shoot unless you have a clue what you're shooting at, God damn it!"

The hidden vehicle stopped. The engine sound settled to a growling idle.

"Ladies and gentlemen of the University of New Mexico Enclave." The voice of Colonel George Donelson boomed from speakers hidden among the derelict buildings outside the wire. "We have generously offered to accept you back into the United States of America under amnesty conditions. You have chosen to hold out. Fine. Now, you're about to witness an object lesson on the downside of treason."

Somewhere a hand hit a switch. An electrical impulse altered the crystalline structure of the sheet of optical-polymer armor. It turned instantly transparent.

A bulldozer with its driver enclosed in transparent bubble armor sat straddling the Lomas median. The shield was supported at the bottom by struts that held it about two meters in front of the blade. An "X" of steel girders, red with rust, had been fixed to the blade. Keith Tauber hung from the cross, clad only in a pair of blue underpants. Steel rods had been ground sharp on one end and welded to the girders at the ends, projecting forward. Tauber's wrists and feet had been impaled on these, and the ends hammered over to secure him. His head hung forward, white-blond hair obscuring his face.

A pair of men in SP cammies slid forward along the sides of the bulldozer. The sheet of bulletproof polymer protected them from sniper fire that began to pop from the Enclave lines without an order from Virág. She did not order it stopped.

One of the SPs threw a bucket of water in Tauber's face. He stirred. The SP grabbed his elbow and tugged.

Tauber's scream rang like a bell across the mist and engine mutter.

"Now," Donelson's amplified voice said, "this unfortunate young man compounded his treason against his country by attempting to betray his fellow rebels. Frankly, I'm shocked and appalled at such behavior. You may think of this as us cleaning *your* dirty laundry. It's all part of restoring law and order to this great land of ours. Gentlemen, you may commence the lesson."

The other SP raised a sledgehammer and shattered Tauber's right knee.

"Am I getting heavy?" Dameron Crowe asked. He sat astride Donovan Steele's broad shoulders. He had his belt on the outside of his plaid jacket, and his crutches and assorted other implements stuck through it in back. The desert wind, still night cool, riffled his mouse-colored hair.

Steele glanced up at the Manzano Mountains. The sky was almost daylight blue, but as close as they were the sun had yet to appear from behind the peaks.

"Not really. But you seem to be pinching a muscle in my neck a little."

"Tough titty. You're the superman, I'm the cripple. You get to carry me. That's life."

Steele laughed. "Hey, cut me some slack. I'm disabled, too, remember? I just have a fancier prosthesis."

"Whoa? What is this? Did Sergeant Dirk Dagger of New York's élite Strike Force crack a *joke?* Jesus. Maybe there's hope you'll turn into a real human being someday."

"I've given up hope of that," Steele said bitterly.

"Chill out," Crowe said. "I wasn't referring to your replacement parts. Face it; you were a killer robot long before the CIA started messing with your head."

Steele started to glare back over his shoulder. To his surprise, his expression turned into a sour grin. To heap verbal abuse on a man who could kick you for a long-range field goal took a great deal of something—balls, or the kind self-hating bravado that leads you to dance on the edge of the cliff in the hope and expectation that one day you'll fall off.

One thing was certain: it was not an excess of stupidity. Tiny, crippled Crowe was in his own way one of the most formidable men Steele had ever met. He was glad the dwarf was on his side . . . for whatever reason, and for however long.

He trudged up a rise like a frozen sea swell, the kind of undulation of this short-grass desert that used to make it possible for Apache war parties to lie in ambush until the cavalry was right on top of them. The land looks flat, but is anything but.

"Well, well, well," Crowe said as they reached the top. "What have we here? It looks very much like an arroyo filled with freshly turned earth. And, brother, let me promise you, this *caliche* ain't turned very easily. Which, presumably, is why that bulldozer is still parked there at the head of the cut."

Steele lowered Crowe to the ground, supported him while he unlimbered his crutches. "I wonder if we can use the dozer."

"And the answer is fuck negatory, buddy boy. Somebody might hear." Leaning one crutch against his hip he reached behind his back and produced an entrenching tool. "And what's this 'we' shit? I'm a cripple; *you're* fusion powered."

Major General Paul Whiteman, USAF, was not an early riser. Reveille was always a sorer trial for him than for his comrades in arms, and he was always mildly surprised he had survived the years of enforced awakening until he attained sufficient rank to sleep as late as he damned well pleased. He put in late hours. He just couldn't *function* in the morning.

When a rapping at the door of his quarters roused him, he knew instinctively it was important. He would never dream of chewing out a subordinate who disturbed him for something trivial. He just made his disappointment known. That was enough to keep it from happening very often. A disappointed general is not a pretty sight.

He was shrugging into his regulation dark blue dressing gown as the regulation blue scuff slippers on his feet flopped their way to the door. "All right, I'm coming," he said. "You don't have to knock the door down." Even understanding, sensitive generals get testy when awakened early.

"What is it?" the general asked, opening the door. There was something familiar about the face of the Security Police sergeant who stood outside. It was handsome in a brutally direct kind of way.

The sergeant held up his right hand, and for a weird dizzy moment Whiteman wondered if the man were showing him a stigma. "Actually, General, it's a gun," the man in the sergeant's uniform said. Whiteman realized that though the hand was blistered the hole in the palm was black with no trace of red. "It's a 10mm, semi-automatic, and built right into my arm. I'm Donovan Steele."

A remarkable figure appeared from behind the cyborg, a tiny man on crutches dressed like a used-car salesman. "And I'm his associate, Dameron Crowe. You can think of us as the Gibson and Glover of the twenty-first century."

"What do you want of me?" the general stammered.

"We want to show you something," Steele said.

"Dead bodies in an arroyo," the general said, pressing his handkerchief over his nose. "It's terrible. But what has it got to do with me? Or with your ridiculous allegations against Colonel Donelson?"

"We're on the base here, are we not, General?" Steele asked.

"Certainly. But it's a big military reservation, and even with the 223rd Special Group on hand, we cannot maintain perfect security. No doubt these are the victims of some biker gang, or those zealots with their illuminated plastic Jesus up in the foothills. Still, so *many*—"

"Yeah," Dameron Crowe said. "Hold that thought. And while you're doing that, take a good look at those bodies, General."

"I hardly see—dear God, can it be possible? There—that woman there, in the lavender sweater, with the bright red hair. That's Patricia Jackson! I *know* her. She used to be first viola with the Albuquerque Symphony Orchestra. She had remarkably supple wrists."

"Well, they've stiffened up some," Crowe observed.

"And there—that's Matt, Matt Carnes, the community activist! And Ralph and Kathy Izard, John and Gail Miller—dear God in heaven, these are people I knew and cherished, people I sat next to at concerts, drank mineral water and ate cheese with at gallery openings and fund-raisers. They're the cream of Four Hills society!"

"When did you last see these people, General?" Steele asked.

"Why, it was right after we recovered the Southeast district. I addressed the population, and then a number of leading citizens—my God, these very people!—their names were on a civic commendation list I myself helped prepare. They were led away and put in trucks, to attend a briefing session on the future of. . . ."

His voice trailed away. "Discussions about their future woulda definitely been brief," Crowe said, lighting a slim brown cigar. "You can sure say that."

"And who took charge of them after they got into the trucks?" Steele asked.

"George." It came out in a whisper. The general raised his round face then, and his eyes shone with grief and rage and shame. "Colonel George Donelson!"

Keith Tauber hung limp on his St. Andrew's cross, his limbs shattered, his body a Jackson Pollock composition all in red.

One of the torturers had disappeared behind the bulldozer. He came back, dragging the oxygen and acetylene tanks of a welding rig on a dolly. He had a welder's mask tipped up on his head, so that it stuck out like the bill of a baseball cap.

"Now we're all about to discover just what kind of balls an Enclave man really has," the Colonel's voice boomed from the hidden speakers. "I think you'll enjoy this little variation, ladies and gentlemen."

The SP with the mask held an electric igniter wand before the nozzle of his torch. He pressed the stud. Yellow flame hissed out.

A burst of 30mm grenades from Janet Virág's Belgian-made launcher, fired at an extremely high angle, dropped neatly behind the transparent polymer shield. Keith Tauber's head and shoulders were shattered. The Blue Beret who was just standing and watching dropped like a marionette with its strings cut.

The oxyacetylene tanks blew with a white flash. The SP with the welder's gear screamed shrilly as flame enveloped him. He staggered out from behind the shield, blazing brightly, shrieking insanely.

"*Let the fucker burn!*" Janet Virág screamed. It was too late. Every defender in sight cut loose on the flaming torturer with whatever came to hand. He danced backward briefly and collapsed into a pile of burning debris that suggested nothing human.

Colonel George Donelson hit the suppress button of his microphone. "Bitch," he said.

He let the button go. "Ingenious," he told the defenders. "Very ingenious. But I'm afraid it's all for naught. You see, I was trying to go *easy* on you. But since you didn't want to sit still for the end of your lesson. . . ."

The defenders snapped out of spectator mode to dive for cover as a barrage of 82mm mortar rounds came whistling down the sky.

Sparks jetted from beneath the snout of the burning Marauder as the bulldozer pushing it from behind ground it into the pavement. The armored car had actually breached the Enclave's barricade across Lomas before a barrage of M-91s had halted it. The base forces' third assault was the most determined yet. At the spearhead the dozer, its driver protected by the polymer-armor bubble, was trying to clear the blazing car out of the way and open a gaping hole in the Enclave perimeter.

Janet Virág burst out of cover. She immediately dived and rolled to avoid a machine-gun burst from a sniper in the phony bell tower of the middle school across Girard. A burst of 25mm cracked like thunder over her head. The Kirtland boys were pouring the coal on, raking the area just inside the gate, pushing hard to secure their breakthrough.

The dozer was a combat model, with a massively armored engine compartment. She shouldered the launcher, centered the aiming dot on the driver's bubble as the huge machine groaned through the wire.

The rocket whooshed away. The bubble lit up from inside with hellish white light as incandescent copper hit the driver like a blowtorch.

A mortar barrage landed all around Virág, filling her head with volcano roaring and rolling her over the pavement like a tumbleweed. She tried to tuck herself into a ball to protect her head and joints, but the dynamic overpressure fronts of 82mm explosions tossed her this way and that and left her sprawled.

The dozer driver was dead. But one of Donelson's smart boys had disabled the dead-man throttle. The machine ground inexorably on, pushing the abandoned Marauder out of the way, rolling on down Lomas, leaving a gaping hole in the wire in its wake.

Virág could barely hear the hoarse shouts as base soldiers charged the breach. She groaned. She pulled her grenade launcher around on its sling to where she could get a grip on it, tried to pick herself up.

A flurry of machine-gun bullets splashed over her, driving her back down to the street and forcing the breath from her body. The polyceram mesh and nysteel inserts kept them from penetrating—or maybe they didn't; it hurt like hell, she was too numb to know for sure, and she wasn't even sure it mattered. Dying of a bullet wound here facing the wrong way on the westbound side of Lomas was a lot nicer prospect than being captured alive. . . .

Figures appeared in the breach, bulky and faceless in assault armor, firing from the hip. Virág skinned her lips back from her teeth in a snarling grin: *Let's see how those* gadjo *bastards like all that neat armor when they're trapped inside it with a bunch of white phosphorus flakes.* Her finger tightened on the trigger.

And a voice boomed down out of the sky: "THIS IS MAJOR GENERAL PAUL WHITEMAN. ALL KIRTLAND BASE PERSONNEL, CEASE FIRE IMMEDIATELY, IN THE NAME OF THE UNITED STATES OF AMERICA!"

13

The hell of fire and noise cut off as if a switch had been thrown. The assault force streaming into the gate stopped, dithered, and then recoiled back outside the wire where they went to the ground, afraid to be stuck inside the enemy perimeter without support.

Virág made herself sit up. It felt as if her every rib were broken, and each sent its own dagger of pain through her lungs. She shouted, "Cease fire!" too, but she might as well have saved herself the pain. None of her people were shooting now either.

A Hummer rolled north into the intersection of Girard and Lomas, into the very eye of the now-quiescent firestorm. A big balloon speaker bobbed behind on a tether. Standing erect behind the machine-gun mount was Major General Paul Whiteman. At the wheel was Donovan Steele.

"THERE HAS BEEN A TERRIBLE MISTAKE," Whiteman's electronically amplified voice said, at once sad and stern. "THE INSTRUMENT THAT WAS TO HAVE BEEN USED TO DRAW TOGETHER A CITY TORN BY STRIFE AND ANARCHY HAS BEEN USED FOR TERRIBLE PURPOSES. LAY DOWN YOUR ARMS. THE FIGHT IS OVER."

His face greenish with fury behind its light dusting of freckles, Colonel George Donelson grabbed his own mike. "The good general obviously can't stand the heat," he said, "so it's time to take him out of the kitchen. Fire the traitor up, boys!"

A moment of confusion as Donelson's troopies stared at one another. Then the Blue Beret machine gunner in the middle school tower opened up on the Hummer.

Bullets gouged asphalt all around the desert-camouflaged car. Steele pushed the general down and stood over him, swinging an M-27 up to his hip. Lasers flashed from his eyes.

A burst slashed across Steele's chest. It stung like a splash of acid. Steele roared and fired a burst. Guided by his sighting lasers, he put two rounds through the gunner's face, below the brim of his helmet. The machine-gun's barrel tipped toward the sky.

Steele's head rocked as a bullet impact hacked open his cheek. He turned. His IR vision caught a funnel of hot muzzle exhaust, expanding in the still-cool morning air, traced it back to its source. Sighting lasers locked on. Steele fired once, and a prone rifleman's brains sprayed over the back of his cammie blouse.

Bullets struck him in chest, belly, thighs. He put a hand out to steady himself against the rollbar; he didn't need two to shoot with, that was just an expert shooter's reflex. Time and again his vision reached out and touched a Blue Beret rifleman, and bullets followed a heartbeat later.

A burst of 25 mike-mike hit him high. He somersaulted over the tailgate of the Hummer. Fortunately the shells weren't armor-piercing. They were merely high explosive; they messed up his organic parts pretty well, but they didn't scratch anything *vital*.

His assault rifle had been knocked away. He rolled to his belly, hauling out his sidearm, a replica Desert Eagle .44 Magnum that Virág had given him in appreciation for services rendered. His flesh-clad fingers were slippery with blood. He had to use both hands this time, to make sure of his grip.

He looked past the Hummer. A Marauder had fired on him up from hull-down position behind the cinderblock wall of a house east of the middle school. Its commander was hunched low in the cupola, fingers hovering over the firing switch. He had seen his target go down. Instead of firing on the Hummer and the concealed general, he was dithering, looking for a fresh target. Steele's lasers found his face.

Steele fired once.

As the Marauder commander's body fell flopping into the turret of his car, the volume of firing rose perceptibly. But nobody was shooting at the general's Hummer or Steele any more, it seemed. The regular Army troops, always a majority of Donelson's forces, had awakened first to their duty to their commanding general, and second to an opportunity to get the spit-shined boots of the 223rd Special Security Group weenies off their necks for good. They had obeyed Whiteman's initial order to cease fire. Now they were opening up again—on the SPs beside them.

Cries sounded from the south side of Lomas:

"Army, *yo!*"

"Hard *core!*"

"Aw*right!* Let's kick us some Blue Beanie *butt!*"

Troops in SP cammies came boiling into Lomas from the yards and houses on the south side, some firing back at their former positions, others tossing away their weapons and going assholes-and-elbows for the wide street's far side. Donelson had left a couple hundred Army troops, mostly those whose loyalty to him he doubted most, behind on base as reserves and security forces. While after two post-Eruption years at Kirtland, they had no reason to love anybody in an Air Force uniform, Whiteman was their legal commanding officer. And when he called for volunteers to bring the renegade Colonel Donelson to heel, very few had hung back. They had convoyed up with Steele and the general, and Whiteman had waited for them to deploy before making his appearance.

Now they were hitting the 223rd SSG in the flank and rear even as their buddies in the ranks were turning on the hated SPs. It was all over in less than a minute.

"Don! *Donnie!* Oh my God, what's happened to you?" Jilly Romero came flying out of the breach the armored car and the bulldozer had torn in the Enclave gate and molded herself to Donovan Steele.

Steele tried to hold her off. "Easy now, babe. I'm fine. Better not hug me; you'll get blood all over you."

"Screw that," Jilly said, and hugged him fiercely.

"You look like an 'after' picture from one of the *Living Dead* flicks," Janet Virág said.

Steele returned Jilly's hug with exaggerated eggshell care. The flesh part of him had sustained horrible damage, and the only way he could endure the yammer of torn nerves was to cut out tactile input to his brain. If he wasn't careful he could snap the girl's spine with an affectionate squeeze.

All around them Army troops were herding 223rd Special Security Groupies around with their hands behind their necks. "You don't look too much like a cover girl yourself," he told Virág, "unless it's on *Soldier of Fortune*."

Virág laughed. One side of her face was bruised and blood soaked her black Virus-7 tee-shirt. "I'll survive. I been through worse. But boy, is Doc Ngoya gonna be pissed when she gets a load of you."

Dr. Jabrandar Singh came through the gate, immaculately dressed, beard trimmed to perfection, turbaned head held high. Instinctively Virág gravitated to his side. She held her FN grenade launcher ready, not entirely trusting the unexpected turn of events that had saved the Enclave from being overrun.

General Whiteman strode to meet him, beaming all over his face. "Dr. Singh! So excellent to see you again."

Surveying the carnage at the intersection, the broken bodies and burning cars, Singh shook the proffered hand. "I might say the same. I only wish we had seen you sooner."

"I'm so sorry. Colonel Donelson just completely pulled the wool over my eyes. The reunification of Albuquerque seemed such noble work. It never occurred to me he might use such ignoble means to achieve it."

"Just where is that motherfucker?" Virág asked. Whiteman's eyebrows rose.

Steele edged her aside. Diplomacy was not her strong suit. "He appears to have pulled out in his command car. Nobody's seen him."

"I'm not gonna rest until that fucker's history," Virág said. For emphasis she checked the LCD panel of her launcher to make sure it was locked, loaded, and fully charged.

Steele shrugged. He was exhausted, mentally if not physically. "Donelson's power is broken. He's a fugitive now, just like me."

"Hey, you don't know how reassuring that is. I see what a great job they've done running you down."

Steele laughed and turned away to tuck a stray end of torn intestine back into his body cavity, out of Jilly's sight.

"Despite my regrets, Doctor," Whiteman was saying, "I still feel the reunification of Albuquerque—and the United States—is a worthy goal. I intend to continue working for both."

"I feel they are worthy goals too, General. The Enclave stands ready to rejoin the city, the state, and the nation when its residents can be assured of freedom and just treatment. But that time is not now. We will continue to resist by force any attempts to subdue us by force; look to Colonel Donelson's example if you wonder why. No matter how worthy, no goals justify atrocity and oppression."

"Amen to that," the General said.

"Drive faster, you moron," Colonel George Donelson snarled at the driver of his command car. *If I can only get back to the base in time, I can contain the damage that bleeding-heart fool Whiteman has done. . . .*

"Sir, I'm going as fast as is safe." San Mateo south of Lomas was claimed by Maynet, but in truth it was no-man's-land, owned by the gangs and rubble-runners. The broad street was still largely choked by the rusting hulks of vehicles caught in a terminal traffic jam two years ago, when everybody was trying to escape the wrath of Eruption, the poison gas and the bombs and the glowing clouds that could scour the meat right off your bones. "There's all these dead cars—"

"No excuses!" It took all Donelson's indomitable will to refrain from striking the man, but obviously the mere task of driving taxed his feeble resources. Distracting him would only make the halfwit wreck the vehicle. "No . . . more . . . excuses! Excuses are what destroyed the country. Excuses are what derailed my *successful effort* to—to—"

He couldn't go on. His jaws locked on the words. Briefly he writhed in silent fury in the Hummer's passenger seat, overcome by the way he had been betrayed at every turn.

"Sir," came a timid voice from the rear of the vehicle, "a verti's just rolled in behind us."

"A verti?" Donelson twisted in his seat, trying to get a look out the polymer-armor side port. "I gave no orders for any aircraft—"

He saw the puff of smoke from the rocket pods slung alongside the verti's fuselage.

"I'm alive," the colonel grunted. "I'm *alive*. And where there's life, there's will."

He let himself fall over the roof of the Hummer, which lay on its side. Inside, he heard his driver groan. He smelled burning rubber, heard the crackle of flames. *Got to get away from the car before it blows*, he told himself.

He tried to rise. His right leg buckled beneath him. The ankle seemed to have turned to mush. He couldn't feel anything from the knee down; maybe that was best.

He started scrambling for the side of the street. He would seek cover among the derelict cars. He couldn't hear the verti, could sense no sign of it—and when the tilt-rotor craft were near, you could *feel* them, the pulsating of engines, the downrush of air. Evidently his enemies had flown off, believing him dead.

He laughed. *The fools! Once again they underestimate me! Me, Colonel George Donelson, USAF!* He would show them just how much that cost. . . .

Reaching out, his hand touched something. He stopped. It was a foot, bare except for the thong of a sandal that seemed to have been made from a slice of an automobile tire.

He looked up a skinny leg. An old woman stood there. Her wrinkled Asian face was unreadable.

"Hello," he croaked. "I'm Colonel Donelson. You've got to help me. It's your duty as a citizen of the—"

Behind him a shot snapped. He shrieked as agony exploded in his left leg.

He rolled over, sat up. His left knee was strawberry jelly. He clutched his thigh and bobbed in agony too great for words.

"Wise guy, huh?" Dameron Crowe lowered his right crutch back to the pavement. There was a .22-caliber hole through its rubber tip that matched the entry wound in the back of Donelson's knee. "Predictable is more like it. We figured you'd cut right back for the base. You'd reckon you could patch everything all up. Hubris, they used to call that. Greek heroes used to suffer from it, to feed that pencil-dick ego of yours."

He smiled. It was an ugly, twisted, snaggle-toothed smile. Nonetheless, Colonel Donelson even *in extremis* saw that it bore a lot of similarity to the inhumanly beautiful smile of the artificial woman, Misericordia.

"Wh—what are you going to do to me?"

"Nothing."

Hope welled inside Donelson like the blood from his knee. The man was a dwarf, and a cripple as well. Cripples had no fiber. They were whiners, too obsessed with the bad hand the world had dealt them to have any kind of character at all. Donelson would bend this freak to his iron will, as he had bent that fat imbecile Whiteman. . . .

"But *them*—" Crowe left a crutch leaning against his hip to wave a hand. "*They're* gonna do plenty."

Donelson looked around. He was surrounded by . . . old women. Mostly Asian, probably Vietnamese, all old and slow and bent. Each of them gripped a knife in her wrinkled hand. A knife or a razor or a broken bottle.

"Who are they? What are you talking about?"

"Grannies," Dameron Crowe said. "Grannies of the girls your men raped and murdered, mothers of the men they tortured to death. These aren't your good solid middle-class white Americans; they take little things like the massacre of loved ones *personally*."

He began gimping backward, thump-thump-slide. "You can just think of them as your *worst nightmare*."

Donelson tried to get to his feet. Neither of his legs worked now. He fell hard, skinning his hands. He tried to scrabble away, weeping at the pain when his shattered knee hit pavement.

The grannies closed in. Sunlight glinted on metal and jagged glass.

Colonel George Donelson began to scream.

14

"Oh dear," Dr. Eleanor Ngoya said. "Oh dear, oh dear, oh dear. We give you a marvelous new body, and look what you *do* to it."

"It seemed like the thing to do at the time," Steele said with a rueful grin. He was sitting on a steel surgical table with his legs dangling and his shirt off. He wasn't pretty.

"When you put your ass on the line, honey," Virág said, "sometimes you get it shot off. It wasn't for Steele, the Two Twenty-Third Special Security Group'd have you bent over that table right now taking turns banging that cute black butt of yours."

"I understand that," the doctor said crisply. Her polished teak cheeks were flushed, but it took Steele's heat-sensitive IR vision to tell. "No one is more grateful than I for what Lieutenant Steele has done for us. For what you've done for us, for that matter."

"Any time, babe. Can I smoke in here?"

"My gratitude only extends so far, Ms. Virág."

Ngoya knelt to examine Steele's wounds. "I know as well as anyone exactly what you are, Lieutenant." She pronounced it *leftenant* in British fashion. "Still, it's something of a visceral shock—if you'll pardon the reference—to see you walking around in this condition. You've suffered massive insult to the

105

body cavity and limbs, plus incredible cosmetic damage."

Steele reached to his cheek, winced when his fingers touched cold nysteel laid bare by a bullet. It had taken him several minutes of concentration, with coaching from Jilly, to jimmy the AI routines in his artificial brain to filter out pain but let through pressure feedback and temperature sensations.

"Can you patch me up? I know, it seems a lot to ask after all you've done for me—"

"Pish. It's no bother at all, really. Of course we can patch you, but first we need to see to containing the damage and debriding the wounds. Gangrene is a very real possibility, and if it advances too far we might have to start over from scratch."

She straightened. "Really, you should be in the emergency room, just like a normal battle casualty. What needs to be done now, they do best."

Steele shook his head. "Not while there are *real* battle casualties. This is ugly, and it hurts like hell if I let it, but it isn't life-threatening. I can't take medical attention away from those who really need it."

Dr. Ngoya looked dubious. "Well, we can use broad-spectrum antibiotics, plus self-replicating assemblers specific to some of the more likely infections, but even that won't do much good unless some organ damage is repaired and dead tissue cleared out—"

A knock on the door. Jilly came through before anyone could answer it.

"Don," she said. "You've got to come to Dr. Singh's office. *Right now.*"

"What is it, kid?" he asked.

She could only shake her head.

Dr. Singh had a wall-sized holographic map display behind his desk. It was blank now. The big communications screen on the far wall by the door was live, though.

A man and a woman sat there. The man wore a white suit. The woman had dark hair hanging past her shoulders. She was dressed in a colorful blouse and a peasant-style skirt. Neither the man nor the woman was very large.

"Ah, Mr. Steele," the man said. He had a drawn, bloodless look, and the skin of his face had that sheen that comes of compulsive scrubbing. "We meet at last, if you'll forgive the cliché. At one remove, of course—a situation I intend shortly to correct."

"Who are you?" Steele asked.

"I am Dr. James, currently director of the Los Alamos National Laboratory. This is my ward, Misericordia."

"Hello, Donovan," the woman said in a deep, throaty voice. His first impression had been that she was plain. Now he saw that she was in fact strikingly pretty, and the smile unfolding now was the most beautiful he had ever seen. "I've waited too long."

"What are you talking about?" he demanded.

She gestured at him. "You look terrible, my love. You really must take better care of yourself. For *me*."

Jilly clutched his arm. He patted her hand. "You're both nuts, right? A counselor is what you need, not me."

Dr. James laughed. "Oh, no, Lieutenant. You're exactly what we need. But we're not the only ones who need you; your brother needs you worse."

It seemed as if his nysteel skeleton turned to ice within him. "My what?"

"Your brother. Matrix. He is our quite involuntary guest."

Steele broke into loud laughter. "That's the silliest thing I've heard in my whole life."

Dr. James smiled. "I know someone who can convince you otherwise."

He and the woman vanished. In their place was the face of Donovan Steele.

Jilly gasped. "Holy shit," Virág said.

Steele shook his head. "No, James, forget all about it. You couldn't possibly be holding Matrix captive. He doesn't even have a *body*. No audioanimatronic Disney phony is going to—"

"Sorry, Don."

The voice shut him up. It was his voice. But it wasn't, not quite. There was a different intonation, dry, slightly acerbic, that didn't belong to him. Or, at least, not to the *him* who was standing staring in shock at a screen in Dr. Jabrandar Singh's office.

"It's me, all right. It's a hell of an irony, isn't it? You wanted your old body back; *I* wanted to transcend the physical plane entirely. So which one of us winds up in an all-organic Donovan Steele body?" He grinned sourly, shook his head.

"But, but *how*—"

"It was simple, I'm afraid. But forget about that. You're going to be tempted to come after me, Don, I know you. *Don't do it*. Understand, it's *what they want*—"

The picture flashed back to Dr. James and the woman. "Your brother is absolutely right," Dr. James said. "It is what we want. We're looking forward to seeing you soon, Lieutenant Steele."

PART TWO

DREAMS IN THE DARK

_15_

"I see you, Donovan," the woman called. She took a final bite from her apple and tossed the core into the lava. "You might as well come out."

Steele had the gain on his hearing turned high, making use of an AI filter to suppress most of the murmur and crackle of the molten stone that flowed, brilliant yellow against the night, between his hiding place and the point where the slim young woman had just stood up. It was a risky ploy, computer filtering; you could never be entirely sure what stray sounds the artificial intelligence was going to decide were volcanic and scrub out of the input you actually heard.

In the event it hadn't mattered. She had not been moving. She had been crouching immobile in wait behind a cluster of black spongy-looking boulders—long-cooled lava, souvenir of the Valle Grande volcano's last hit performance a million years ago.

He slipped his rucksack off and stood up from the boulders and the stunted scrub that somehow survived the heat and toxic gases. She was scarcely thirty meters away across a ten-meter-wide river of fire, seeming to shimmer in the heat that pushed at him like a physical force. She appeared unarmed. He held his own M-27 lightly in the patrol position, slanted across his hips.

She clapped her hands delightedly. "Oh, it's true! They put the meat back on your bones at the Enclave. We figured that must have happened, when we started hearing descriptions of this 'Peter Murphy' who was supposed to be speaking for you."

"So you're Misericordia."

She nodded. In the yellow glare her skin had an odd texture, almost as if she were wearing thick full-body makeup.

"You see into the infrared spectrum, don't you?" he asked.

"Of course."

"So I know how you saw me approach. How come I didn't see you waiting there, against the hillside?"

She bent slightly to the side, reached down. Steele started to twitch up his rifle. She grinned, raised a bucket of water, poured it over herself. The "makeup" began to sluice away.

"It's a paste made out of volcanic ash and water," she said, scrubbing the stuff off with her hands. "Basically mud. Very good insulation. So near the lava flow I judged you would not be able to separate my heat signature and exhalations from the background."

Steele pulled his head back on his neck. "You have a pretty accurate idea of my capabilities."

She smiled. "Of course. I'm your biggest fan." She finished wiping away as much of her insulative coating as she was going to get, stood up straight. With a mild shock he realized she was nude.

"How'd you know I'd come here?" he asked.

"I didn't, for sure. The volcano cut all the land routes onto Pajarito Plateau, and Dr. James has refused to try to restore any of them. It gives him a feeling of security. This is the narrowest part of the flow." She shrugged. "I thought I'd see you here, sooner or later."

"So what happens now? You call the patrols to try to pick me up?"

She laughed. "Call them how? As good as I am, I'm not psychic." She held her hands out from her sides. "And I could hardly be carrying a concealed transmitter."

That wasn't strictly true. Steele let it go.

"Besides," she said, "there aren't any patrols. Just me."

Steele's face registered the surprise he felt. "I thought I was being lured here so Dr. James could get hold of me."

She frowned. "You were brought here for *me*. Nothing else."

She turned and sprang up the steep slope, bouncing from outcroppings like a mountain goat. Steele whipped up the M-27, fired a single shot. The slim pale form suddenly darted right, even as his finger tightened on the trigger. Despite having a lock with his sighting lasers, he missed by half a meter.

He tried again, making sure to lead her with what both his sighting subroutines and his own experienced shooter's eye told him was exactly the right amount. As the shot cracked off, she froze like a lizard on a rock. The 4.77mm bullet splintered black stone three fingers above her head.

Frustrated, Steele switched the weapon to full-auto and let loose a burst. Misericordia slipped around a hip of ground into a hidden crevice.

"See you up top," she called. "I'll be waiting for you, my love." Then all that was left was her laughter, dancing like a tinsel strand in the turbulent updrafts off the Hell-hot glowing flow.

Steele hunkered back down into cover, unwilling to take everything she said at face value. The plateau loomed above him like a derelict battleship, beached and long ago abandoned. No lights showed, no motion; Steele could hear nothing but the grumble of the lava. As far as his artificially enhanced senses could discern there was no life at all on the plateau.

He stood. He threw the rucksack underhand across the flow. Then he slung his rifle over his back, backed up several steps, and took a run at the molten river.

A stone turned beneath his foot as he launched himself. He had been good at track in school, and the additional power his enhancements gave him offered him what he hoped was a margin of safety. For a moment it felt as if he were bathing in live steam. Then the other bank was coming up—short.

His feet touched solid earth. With all his fusion-driven strength he snapped his body forward, desperately trying to impart the last slice of forward momentum. For a moment he balanced there, on the brink, and then he toppled forward.

The earth seemed blessedly cool. He lay there for a long moment savoring the earth's embrace and breathing in the sulfur. Not even his nysteel skeleton would survive immersion in the devil's torrent that was cooking his soles through his boots.

He picked himself up and dusted himself off. His bandages were coming loose again. He brushed what dirt he could away, but it was a losing effort. Dr. Ngoya was going to have her work cut out for her when he got back to the Enclave.

Only a long habit of absolute self-discipline in the kill zone kept him from laughing out loud at his newly discovered gift for self-deception. He wasn't likely to be returning to the UNM Enclave. Not in this incarnation.

He shouldered his pack and started up the slope.

At the top he crouched low and peered around. He could not detect the woman directly with any sense he had. But she had left tracks in a fresh fall of ash like new snow. He smiled sourly and cautiously moved out.

He wasn't too sure what had been on top of Pajarito Plateau before Eruption. He had the idea that civilians had largely been cleared out of Los Alamos and environs in the early twenty-first century, under the guise of reclaiming the environment of the scenic Jemez Mountains. Of course, it had mainly been to cover an expansive new phase of hyper-secret defense research at the National Labs, after people finally figured out that history wasn't going to go away just because the Soviets had.

The highest mountain in the Jemez was Redondo Peak, but the range's most striking characteristic was a hole: the *Valle Grande*, Big Valley in Spanish, a grassy, gently sloping bowl eighteen miles by twelve. The largest extinct volcano on Earth.

The largest *formerly* extinct volcano on Earth. The *Valle* had come to life again with a bang two years before and reclaimed the Jemez environment for itself.

What the plateau's top looked like, mostly, was as if the Devil had decided to build an annex to Hell, and let the job out to the lowest bidder. The volcano's initial explosions had knocked down most of whatever was standing. It scoured the remains with "glowing clouds," fluid masses of white-hot ash— mobile firestorms that moved at the speed of sound, the things that killed Pompeii and St. Pierre. Then it dumped tons of ash and torrential rains on everything.

Donovan Steele moved among shapes that suggested almost

nothing to a sane mind. Even with his enhanced senses he could barely make sense of the scene. He picked his way over low ridges, sporadically spiky and strangely parallel. Not until he accidentally hit one with his foot and then crouched low behind it in case the noise drew fire did he realize that it was a pine, knocked flat by a blast.

He passed between low humped shapes and taller geometric shapes. They must have been buildings, some of which had survived the volcano's buffeting more intact than others. They .were all coated in a stucco-like coating of dried ash-mud, what Misericordia had used to hide herself from his heat-sensing ability. It robbed them of outline, of identity, made one shape flow into the next without revealing clearly what it was or had been.

Around him the volcano made its noises, like a dragon in fitful sleep.

The tracks wound between obstacles in a generally north-westerly direction. Steele followed them without difficulty. He moved purposefully but without haste, alert to the possibility that his quarry—or was she the hunter?—might have doubled back on him and be lying in ambush somewhere in this melted-Cubist landscape.

He had listened to her breathing, and had some of the handy little AI helpers in his brain keyed to recognize its signature patterns. It should help him detect her if she was lying in wait by the path. But nothing was infallible.

The path wound around a place where a tall Ponderosa pine had been knocked down onto a blocky building and then covered with mud and ash, creating a surrealistic lean-to effect. Ahead the plateau opened up. Steele suddenly pressed himself to the flank of the ruined building and knelt.

She was clearly visible ahead. She was seated on a rock on the cliff's edge not twenty meters away, facing away from him, her bare back a pale glimmer in the starlight. With his infrared vision he could literally see the heat rising from the lava two hundred feet below.

Moving with exaggerated care he raised the rifle. It was too damned bad; something in him rebelled at the idea of shooting a woman, especially one this beautiful. Shooting her in the back didn't help.

But he wasn't sure, really, that this *was* a woman. And the old Strike Force cop in him said it didn't really matter anyway. She was just another sociopathic perp, as deadly and unreasoning as a screamer far gone in the grip of Virus-3. The only thing you could do with that kind was take them out as cleanly as possible.

He reached out with his lasers, locked, took a deep breath, released half of it, and fired.

She vanished. Even as the rifle came back down on line he knew in his mortifying guts that he hadn't hit her. She'd dropped *as* he shot.

He scanned the rocks where she'd disappeared. Whatever she was she had senses as taut and sensitive as the skin of a bubble, and reflexes close to the speed of light.

A flash, slightly to his left. Before he could track the piece around, an impact torqued it savagely in his hands. Fingers stinging from the vibrations, he tried to bring the rifle to bear, but a second shot knocked the box magazine out from behind the pistol grip, and a third smashed the receiver and stung his cheek with metal splinters.

"Step away from the building, Donovan," the woman called.

Mindful of her inhuman senses he suppressed a smile, *Might as well play along.* He stood.

"Throw away the rifle." He did so. "Now lose your sidearm and your knives. Oh, and there's an armor-piercing grenade in the under-barrel launcher attached to my rifle, in case you're getting smug."

He obeyed. He was not particularly worried. He was reasonably confident he would not be a much easier target for her than she was for him—and launched grenades were slow, which meant a relatively long flight time for his enhanced reflexes to play around in. He wanted to see where she was leading, and besides he had more than a few options left.

Also, he found he didn't particularly care about the outcome one way or another. He was tired. Life since he reawakened in the foothill Fortress of Faith among the fanatic followers of the Church of Christ in Living Color had been constant strife. Since the warehouse ambush, in fact—hell, as long as he could remember.

He would hate to let Matrix down. But he knew his chances of somehow freeing his brother—actually a backup copy of his personality, made by Project Download scientists and inadvertently allowed to escape—were microscopic. Steele could not even guess how James could catch and hold a being like Matrix, who was pure electronic impulses and who could move and operate even along plain electric wires.

He would play this hand without regrets, without concern for his own survival, which had grown to be a burden to him anyway. He had entered a state the Japanese call "living as one already dead." It made him even more dangerous.

"Step on out here in the open with your hands behind your neck," Misericordia commanded. "That's right. Come closer, now. By the way, I know about the pistol built into your right arm, darling. I know everything about you."

"I'm usually picky about who calls me 'darling,'" he said easily. "For starters, I usually insist they be human."

She laughed. "You're trying to provoke me! How sweet. It won't work. I'm more than human, and proud of it. You would be too, if you thought about it—proud of what you are, I mean."

"I'm what they made me," he said flatly. "Just like you. I had nothing to do with it."

"Everybody is what they're made—and what they make themselves. It isn't just your nysteel skeleton and your fusion-generator heart that make you what you are, my love."

"I wish you'd stop calling me that. I'm not anything except your prisoner, at the moment. So what's it to be? Are you going to shoot me, or just take me below?"

"What fun would that be? I told you, you're *mine*." She turned and threw the assault rifle over the cliff. It cartwheeled down into the lava, raising barely a splash in the dense superheated molten rock.

She turned, raised her hands in a mantis fighting stance. "All right. Take me now."

"You must be kidding."

She smiled.

"Listen," he said, lowering his hands from behind his neck. Down in the glowing stone river a gas bubble popped with a sound that rumbled deep in his torn and tortured belly. "This is crazy. A woman doesn't have upper body strength to compare to a man's, especially one my size. And I don't care what kind of gene-engineering wizardry went into your creation, nothing of flesh and blood can match the power my nysteel augments give me."

A whirlwind of motion. He had just started to react, to try to dance back and block, when his head was snapped around by a spinning back kick.

Then she was standing in front of him again, hands up and weaving gently at the ready, smiling at him. "You think it's a mismatch, do you, darling?"

He felt something crawling on his upper lip. He brushed at it with his thumb. The thumb came away black and shiny wet with blood.

Misericordia wrinkled her nose. "You're hot. You've got a hell of a fever, and from the smell you've got a lot of tissue mortification in your body cavity, hon. If you were human you'd be dead in a few hours from peritonitis. You should take better care of yourself."

"I didn't have time to get patched up properly after the fight at the Enclave." He'd been dosing himself with the antibiotics and antipathogens Ngoya had given him, but she'd told him they would mostly be useful for helping him deceive himself.

With sudden decision he snapped up his right arm, palm out, fired a shot into her sternum. But she wasn't there. She had danced left, and in, seizing his wrist in slim steel-strong fingers.

As the 10mm fired she spun clockwise, throwing her back against his elbow. She was incredibly massive for her size; the joint locked. Before Steele could pull away she uttered a glass-shattering scream and smashed a backfist against the locked elbow.

With a shriek of tortured nysteel the joint popped.

He felt no pain—no nerve-endings in nysteel—but the shock went through him like a bullet in the guts. He tore his arm free by sheer wild strength, lashed a knife-hand blow with his good arm. Stiffened fingers brushed her cheek as she sprang back, laid it open like a blade.

Then she was facing him again, tipping her head to the side so that the blood ran to her mouth. She licked it hungrily from her lips.

Donovan Steele held up his right arm in disbelief. The forearm hung slack. He could move the fingers, he could still fire the integral pistol. But the joint was blown out.

"That took everything I have, darling," she said, breathing heavily. The gash in her cheek was closing as Steele watched. "You're right about strength. You *are* stronger, a lot stronger. But I'm quicker. And unlike you, I was designed to be a killer from the ground up. I'm not an after-market upgrade."

He stared at her. He was starting to wonder if maybe she *wasn't* crazy. Or, at least, wasn't delusional. She could be the most lethal opponent he had ever faced, this slender beautiful woman with the soul-rending smile. She was not made of bullet-proof nysteel, like Stalker, and she didn't have a plasma projector built into her arm, as Stalker had. But Stalker *had* been crazy, had been all but totally dysfunctional mentally. In the end he fought Steele in blind berserk rage, and that destroyed him.

However twisted it was, the mind of the woman who called herself Misericordia functioned as perfectly as her body.

"What do you want?" he asked.

"I want you. I want you to take me. Isn't that what the heroine always wants, in those barbarian comics and after-the-holocaust video shows? A real man who can take them by force?

"I don't *want* a real man. I've had plenty. They aren't good enough to truly take me. Only you are, Steele. Only you in the world."

He charged, stutter-stepping forward and firing a front-snap kick with superhuman speed. She skipped back, effortlessly keeping the same distance between them.

Steele started edging in on her more deliberately. Smiling, she let him come. Her nipples were erect, nostrils delicately flared.

He feinted a punch at her face, then dropped and spun clockwise, scything a savage sweeping kick at her legs. She leapt above his outstretched right leg in an effortless *pas de chat*.

It was a set-up. He lunged, driving a punch at her in midair that would drive his fist right through that perfect belly of hers and out her back.

She slapped her hands around his fist, rode the blow away, sailed backwards through the air to land laughing on the very brink of the cliff.

Her laughter quickly died. The lava had undercut the plateau here. She stood on an outcrop poised above the river of glowing fluid stone with only sulfur-stinking air to three sides of her. As the realization dawned her smile curdled like milk.

He closed again, deliberately. He had her now, pinned with her back to the edge of the cliff. If she didn't have room to use her lightning-swift mobility, his superior mass and strength could take effect.

She jumped onto a black rugged boulder jutting over the very lip of the precipice and threw her arms out to her sides.

"Take me," she cried, head back, eyes closed. "You've got me. *Take me*."

Steele grabbed. He knew her implied surrender was another crazy-cunning ploy; it wouldn't work this time. He was concerned to get right up on top of her, immobilize her arms. Then he could simply pick her up and carry her away no matter how she struggled.

Because there was no pain he forgot his right arm was useless. Misericordia did not. As his hand came flopping through the air like a wingshot pigeon, she grabbed it, turned, ducked, and pulled.

Donovan Steele's greater mass and greater strength translated into great momentum. Under her swift, sure guidance it sent him over her shoulder and into space.

An instant of going end over end, feeling the air rush past. Falling into the furnace heat that welled up from the lava was like falling in slow-motion through a succession of glass panes. It was like physical impacts, brittle somehow and also cutting, that just went on and on.

He heard the mad triumphant laughter of the artificial woman, and then the lava had its way with him.

16

Consciousness returned to Donovan Steele slowly. A particle at a time.

Was it a dream? was his first coherent thought. A dream of falling, falling—he'd had those before. When he was a kid, after his mother had turned into a Screamer and infected his father and two brothers, and his father had had to kill them and then himself before young Donovan's eyes, he'd had nightmares like that often.

I didn't feel a thing when I hit the lava, he thought. *You don't feel anything in dreams*.

He opened his eyes.

He was lying on his side, with the ground cool on his body and cheek. There was something wrong with his vision. He could quite clearly see the short, dry blades of khaki grass waving in the breeze a few inches from his nose. Beyond that the picture became progressively more blurry. He had the impression of tall trees, pines with straight reddish boles shooting up into the sky. But details eluded him.

He stirred, rose somewhat. His body felt good, surprisingly good. There were none of the aches he associated with sleeping on the hard ground. More than that, there was no feeling of suppressed pain, like white noise on a radio turned almost all the way down. It was as if he had never taken repeated gunshot wounds outside the wire at the Girard entrance to the Enclave. Or had that been a dream too?

He got up. Or tried to; for some reason he found himself on all fours. Yet that was in its way reassuring too; his right arm supported his weight, no problem.

So it had been a dream, the nightmare battle on the cliff, the fall into one of Hell's running sores. He grinned. Maybe it was time to head back to the shrinks, if he was going to dream up naked women that incredibly beautiful and then dream about *fighting* them.

He tried to straighten up. His body rose unwillingly to about forty-five degrees, then fell forward again. He frowned. Maybe he had gotten hurt somehow, despite his sense of well-being. Now that he thought about it, he didn't feel entirely right. He felt *good*. Just . . . wrong.

Maybe it was the gray blur at the bottom of his field of vision or his general inability to resolve objects at any kind of distance. Maybe it was the way that the sounds of the woods around him seemed to prick him from all directions like porcupine quills, but softly, not unpleasantly: the wind gently rattling branches and rustling grass, the cry of a hunting hawk, the scurry of insects invisible among the roots of the dry ground cover. Or the odd vividness of the smells of grass and pine forest and the distant but acrid tang of the volcano. Something had been done to his sensory package, as if one sense—sight—had been turned down, and others had been amplified.

He looked at his hands. Shock chilled him like liquid oxygen blasting into his veins.

He had no fingers. His hands were small gray appendages shaped vaguely like aces of clubs. They were vaguely fuzzy.

He looked down at himself. His breastbone was V-shaped, like the keel of a ship. It was covered with shaggy hair, cream-colored around the collarbone, shading to a dirty, streaky gray farther back.

Wildly he turned his head left and right. He was aware of thin hot sunlight and a cool restless wind blowing against large ears set high on his head. He crossed his eyes, concentrated until the blurred grayness at the bottom of his field of vision became a gray snout tapering away, with long fine vibrissa sweeping back to either side.

A dream, yammered in his brain. *It has to be a dream!* Unable to pinch himself, he doubled back and bit his own haunch just ahead of his bushy tail. All it gave him was a pain in the ass.

A coyote! I'm a coyote! Unable to believe, unable to deny, he put back his head and howled at the high uncaring clouds.

Donovan Steele's face turned away from the video screen. "Was that necessary? Putting him in the body of a cyborg coyote, for God's sake?"

"Would you prefer we left him to that?" asked Dr. James, gesturing with a bloodless hand. The huge flatscreen on the wall of the simple bedroom was windowed. To either side of the howling animal's image ancillary views followed Donovan Steele's final plunge into the lava. He hadn't made much of a splash.

"That depends on what you intend to do with him. How'd you pull it off, anyway?"

"Remote Upload. His artificial brain was built with that capability. It was a last line of defense, against the possibility that he might go berserk, as Stalker did—as, indeed, he was accused of doing. Unfortunately—or not, I suppose, depending on one's perspective—none of his antagonists had the knowledge or the equipment to take advantage of that design feature."

He smiled without warmth. "Until now, of course."

The man with Steele's face sighed. "So he never had a chance? It was all a set-up, right from the start. All you had to do was throw a switch and—*whiff*."

"My dear Matrix, did you at any time suspect us of playing *fair?* You should know better by now."

"*I* always play fair," said Misericordia, who stood behind Dr. James's chair eating an ice cream bar. She had on her Gypsy outfit, peasant skirt and bright blouse with matching bandanna. "It's just always fair that I *win*."

Dr. James flicked a glance of irritation over his shoulder at her. "Sometimes, my child, your puerile conceits grow tiresome."

She pouted, very prettily.

Three loud raps sounded, as if a giant were knocking at the door. Matrix stared around, startled and mystified.

"It's nothing," Misericordia said in a bored voice, finishing off her ice cream and licking chocolate off her fingers. "Just the volcano. It makes noises all the time."

"Great. It would be a perfect little irony for me to get a body—which I didn't want to begin with—only to have it crushed or cooked in a volcano."

"You have nothing to fear on that score," Dr. James said. "The volcano has taken its best shot at us long since, and we survived."

"Right." Matrix rubbed his chin. Something rasped. He yanked his hand away in surprise, then realized it was just beard stubble. "So where'd you stick him first? You didn't just pop him into the coyote?"

"No, indeed. As a buffer, initially, we used the Isolated Processing Unit. The very place we trapped and held you, until we found a still more effective means of containment."

Matrix grimaced, looked down at his left hand, which was swathed in bandages. He had all of Donovan Steele's memories up through the point at which his Uploaded mind had been backed up in the secret CIA lab on Basement Level Three of Federal Plaza in New York. But from the instant he had first become self-aware—by a process not even he understood—in the Project Download computer system, he had been conscious of his own identity. Steele's memories were like videos he had watched; vivid, perhaps, but they had happened to someone else. He, Matrix, had never *had* a body.

When he woke up in this all-too-human body he panicked. He tore the cover off the overhead light fixture, broke out the fluorescent bulb, and stuck his hand in the socket. He had already spent maddening months in the containment bottle to which Dr. James had lured him; now all he had to do was get in contact with flowing electric current and he'd be off and running. . . .

All he got for his pains was pain. Burns and a nasty shock. The human body and the human brain were a protoplasmic black box whose workings he could not manipulate. He was trapped.

Rising to go, Dr. James noticed his captive brooding over his bandaged hand. "We can get that seen to, if you'd like."

"No thanks. I prefer to keep it as a reminder of what I've chosen to leave behind."

"Very well." James stood. "You need have no fear that your brother will suffer loss of personality or brain function. Implanted in the coyote's skull is a miniaturized computer brain that's every bit as powerful as the one he was equipped with."

He smiled again. "I want him with all his faculties intact. I have great plans for this brother of yours."

The door opened. Dr. James turned, mouth taut with annoyance. "What is it?"

A man stuck his face in. It was a large face, a bit overlarge for its height off the ground, an odd shiny gray-brown color with cheekbones that seemed to press the eyes up until they turned to crescent slits. "Dr. James. I'm concerned that you're alone with that man."

Misericordia sneered. "He's safe, Tapcis. He's with me, not your clowns."

"You really feel that—*thing*—can keep you safe, Director?" Tapcis asked. He had opened the door enough to reveal a middle-sized body, fit-looking except for a hard little bowling-ball paunch, encased in a dark blue uniform. Two men stood behind him in jumpsuits of the same color, battle rifles clutched in gauntleted hands, faces obscured by the visors of combat helmets.

"Indeed I do. I was just leaving, in any event."

Tapcis turned his slick taupe face to Misericordia. "I have a bone to pick with you. You murdered four of my men."

She pursed her lips. "I was defending myself."

"They were doing their duty."

"It's Dr. James's fault," Misericordia said sulkily. "He wanted to test me."

"You didn't have to kill them! My men aren't just—just sheep for you to slaughter."

She smiled sweetly. "Yes, they are."

Dr. James held his hand up as if to grasp the lab security chief by the upper arm. He stopped short of contact, as if the dark-uniformed man were surrounded by a force field. "Come along now, Major. You have more pressing duties than debating past history."

He escorted Tapcis into the hall. The door slid closed of its own accord. It would only open to someone whose retinal patterns—scanned by invisible low-power lasers—matched those of people it recognized as authorized.

Onscreen the scruffy doglike creature ran from bush to bush, sticking its nose under each and shaking its head. Matrix slumped in his chair. "So why does James even *have* a cyborg coyote, anyway? Where's the point?"

"It's one of his little schemes," Misericordia said. She had her butt propped on a low dresser. "He thinks coyotes would make excellent scouts if you plugged human minds into them. Modularizing the mind; he's real big on that."

"That's the craziest thing I've ever heard."

"Maybe. Dr. James wants to learn all he can about the human mind. Twisting it, turning it, this way and that." She shrugged. "When he's done, he thinks that'll make him God."

She stood up, walked with her hips swinging to the bed, sat down in the middle of it. Her wraparound skirt fell open, making it obvious she was naked beneath. "Would you like to make love to me?" she asked.

He lunged for her throat.

For a while, then, he just lay there stunned at the base of the wall she'd thrown him against. Moving unhurriedly she got up and walked around to bend over him.

"Hon," she said, "my muscles are denser and more efficient than a human's. They're like a chimp's. That's why a seventy-kilo adolescent female chimp is stronger than, say, an offensive tackle. I weigh a bit more even than that, and I'm stronger even than a male chimpanzee."

To emphasize her point she straightened, lifting him to his feet as if he were a child. He made no attempt to resist. The back of his head had taken a nasty crack on the wall, and for the moment coping with the physical world was a bit much for him.

She pushed him down on the bed. "You have Steele's face," she said, "and Steele's body. You even have his mind. But you aren't Steele."

"No." Shaking his head, fingertips to forehead, he tried to sit up. "No, I'm not."

She pushed him back down. "But you're *almost* Steele."

He was wearing blue jeans. She tore the tough fabric at his fly as if it were notepaper. He wore no underwear.

She removed her blouse and skirt, tossed her bandanna aside. She knelt on the bed and bent over him. Her long dark hair cascaded over his hips. She sucked his cock up into her mouth.

After a moment she lifted her head. Her lips shone. "You aren't responding," she said in a husky voice. "Are you afraid?"

He looked at her. She laughed.

"I forgot who you are," she said. "I know I'm good. So the problem is, you're not interested. Right?"

He hesitated, ever so slightly. Even a very brave man hesitates before giving bad news to a person who could pull his head off as readily as she could crack her knuckles.

"No," he said, "I'm not interested. You're beautiful—no denying that. I—I don't belong here. In the physical world, I mean. It's not for me."

"Okay." She got up off the bed, gathered up her clothes, and started for the door.

"Wait," he said. She turned back. "What happens to us now?"

"To you, nothing. You're too dangerous in your information form, and in human form you're not interesting to Dr. James."

"And Donovan?"

She shrugged. "He'll wish we'd let his mind go into the lava with his body," she said. Carrying her clothes, she stepped out into the corridor.

_17_

He became aware of vision. The mountain forest was gone; gone was all sense of smell, of touch, the taste of crisp air on his lolling tongue. There were sounds, but they were dominated by a subliminal background hum of mechanism.

Movement. He tried to focus. He could not seem to move.

A face appeared, a body. Misericordia with her hair hanging unbound around her shoulders, chewing on a protein bar. She raised her fist, made tapping gestures. Steele heard knocking sounds. The sound was flat, lacking life, lacking flavor.

"Are you in there?"

"Yes," a voice said from somewhere. It was his. Not that it was familiar to him. But he was aware of having spoken the word he'd heard.

She glanced away from the invisible partition. "He's awake."

"Where am I now?"

At the woman's side appeared . . . himself. "In the trap they built for me."

For a moment his consciousness just freewheeled. He couldn't assimilate what had happened to him, what was happening. He felt alternately hot and cold.

"Matrix?" he asked.

His head nodded.

"Wh—what are you doing with her?"

Matrix held his hands palms up toward Steele, drew them back in and across his face. "This body was cloned from yours. It has your strength, your reflexes."

A corner of the mouth quirked up. *Do I really grin like that?* Steele wondered. "You know how much good they'd do against this innocent-looking babe here."

Misericordia smirked. "I beat you, Donovan. You were the best, and I beat you."

Panic welled. *"Where am I?"*

"Dr. James—he's the director of the National Labs here—interviewed survivors from Project Download and police and government personnel involved in the hunt for you back in New York when our good friend Senator Bryce Carman was on your case. He also seems to have obtained fragmentary copies of Dev Cooper's personal log. The upshot was, James deduced my existence. He built a trap especially for me. You're in it."

"I don't understand, Matrix. How could *you* be trapped?"

"Like I was a zit-faced teen-aged hacker. It was after the bomb blew your verti to hell in Tijeras Canyon—you did know it was a bomb, didn't you?"

"I figured it out."

"Before the ship's electronics died I was able to tell that you were still among the living—in a kind of fugue state, a coma, maybe, but there was somebody home even if the lights weren't on. I figured the parts of you that wouldn't keep were pretty much beyond repair, so I didn't hurry.

"You were on your way here following up a rumor that they could give you your old, all-natural body back." He smiled and spread his hands. "Good call, Don. Anyway, I started nosing around the systems up here, trying to see if you were right, see if I could turn up something before I brought out a rescue party.

"Now, they have internal scrambling on their data and software here, the kind where, if you don't have the key, it'll take about twice the life span of the solar system to work it out, even with the fastest processors available. Basic security stuff. But I thought I had a line on where I could find the key."

He took a deep breath. "That was the set-up. I came—" He slapped the glass wall with his hand. "—here. This is what Dr.

James calls his Isolated Processing Unit. He built it specifically
for me. It doesn't communicate with the outside world at all.
No outgoing data buses, no outgoing power lines; it has its
own miniature fusion generator, just like you do. He had a
watchdog AI routine in there, keyed to my—our—thought
patterns; Dr. James has got plenty of data on the two of
us. When it sniffed me, the cables I'd come in along were
physically blown loose by explosive charges, and that's all
she wrote."

Steele was confused. He felt anesthetized. Maybe that was
an effect caused by lack of physical stimulus, maybe it was
his mind giving way with the strain.

"Then how did you get out there and me in here?" he
asked.

"Little guy walked in and threw a knife switch. That's the
annoying thing about being a purely electronic life form; little things like mechanical switches are beyond your control.
Blasted about half a megawatt through me. The good doctor
couldn't have known it wouldn't just kill me; I suspect he
didn't much care. But what it turned out to be was the world's
biggest speedball—an incredible rush. I saw God. I *was* God.
But I couldn't function.

"They wheeled in a Donovan Steele clone fresh out of the
deep freeze. There's a complete Download unit attached to
the processor you're in, Don. But it has physical cut-outs—
more knife switches—that I couldn't do anything about. They
rigged up the body, tripped the switches, and blasted me in
here before I could gather my wits."

He held his hands out from his sides. "So here I am,
just another goob off the streets. I do have the body of a
well-trained fighting man, but I don't have much idea what
to do with it. I'm not *you* anymore, Don; I've evolved away
from all this, and it's hard for me to come back."

"How'd they get me in here, if there's no connection to the
outside world?"

"Another little unit they wheel in and hook up by hand.
Has one-way current flow, using Josephson junctions. You
know how they work? Electron tunneling, like in a scanning-
tunneling microscope. You cut a wire in two, slip a perfect
resistor between the ends. Current won't pass through it either
way, right? Wrong. If you apply any voltage, any push, the

resistor cuts off the current. You take away the push, though, and you get a trickle current, one way and one way only. In effect, the electrons teleport to the other side of the resistor. And no matter how much you might want to, *you* can't teleport the other way."

"I don't understand any of this," Steele complained. "It sounds like magic."

"You should have paid more attention to this stuff in school, Don. Then you could operate at a higher level of ignorance."

"Are you men about finished with your technospeak?" Misericordia asked. She was wandering around on her side of the partition gazing at the readouts and displays. Steele had the impression that she was looking at them purely as esthetics, pretty blinky lights, unable to comprehend what they indicated or at least not deigning to.

She came back now with her arms crossed under her small breasts. "Matrix talks a lot more than you do, I bet, Donovan."

"He seems to."

"As I say, I'm not really *you* any more, Don," Matrix said, "even if I do have your body. You can have it back any time, believe me."

The door opened behind Matrix and Misericordia. Dr. James walked in flanked by two of Tapcis's men in battle dress.

"It's time you returned to your quarters, Matrix. These men will escort you."

Matrix turned and suddenly threw himself at Dr. James. Without even glancing aside Misericordia whipped her arm out, caught him by the back of his shirt. She threw him face first into the glass partition. It flexed with a deep booming sound. He slid down it, leaving a smear of blood from his nostrils.

Steele yelled in outrage, static crashing from the speakers of the IPU. Matrix's fingers scrabbled feebly at the glass as Misericordia pulled him to his feet. "Matrix, you are a nice man," she said. "I like you, even if you don't like me. Behave yourself."

She threw him to the heavily armed guards. They took him out, supporting him under the arms.

Steele watched him go, marveling. *He started out as me, but I'm damned if I've looked that clumsy on the attack since I was twelve.* Matrix claimed to have transcended the physical, and what he did with Steele's body and reflexes tended to bear him out.

Still . . . Steele had faced Misericordia with a nysteel skeleton, fusion power, and a gun in his arm, and he'd come out second best. With his natural body, fit and finely honed as it was—if he'd had a body, he would have had to repress a shudder.

Dr. James came to stand right up against the partition with his hands neatly clasped behind his back. "Well, Mr. Steele. At last we find ourselves face to face. Even if you were so ill prepared as to leave your face behind."

"Oliver Higgins mentioned you once or twice," Steele said. "He knew you hated him and hated Project Download. Look, is this still some crazy rivalry? Because if it is, there's just no point—"

Dr. James held up his hand. "Please. Oliver Higgins is dead. He was killed by my good friend Bryce Carman before you dealt with *him* in your own very summary way. With Higgins died Project Download. This isn't personal. This is science."

Steele felt anger, a formless roiling within. His cheeks should have been burning. "That's the biggest crock of shit I've ever heard in my life!" he exploded. "You build some kind of cybernetic mousetrap for my brother, you stick me in the body of a coyote, you keep a freezer full of *clones* of me! Not personal? You're *obsessed* with me."

Misericordia laughed happily. Dr. James glanced at her in annoyance. "I am *fascinated* by you, Steele. You are unique. Oliver Higgins did not simply pull your name out a hat, Lieutenant. He was a fool in many ways, but his selection criteria were immaculate. You were chosen by a most exhaustive selection process for your mental attributes as well as physical."

He began to pace with small neat steps, almost as if he were a marching windup toy. "Think about what you are, what you've done. Not what was done to you. You still retain Downloaded knowledge and skills after more than two years. No other Download recipient has retained the abilities for even six months. Not one. And almost eighty percent of subjects manifested signs of schizophrenia after receiving downloads."

Misericordia slowly clapped her hands. "Bravo, Doctor. Except you're forgetting one Download recipient: me. *I* haven't lost any of my Downloaded traits."

"You're a special case. Also, you're only four months old. Don't interrupt me."

He turned to face the audio-visual pickups of the IPU. "Consider the effects of large-scale cyborging. You underwent to all intents and purposes a full-body replacement. The way you were able to perform in Albuquerque with none of your organic components remaining proved just how vestigial those components were."

"You don't have to remind me," Steele said bitterly. In a way, Albuquerque had confirmed what had been his deepest fear ever since he'd awakened after the Borodini ambush: that he was merely a robot playing at being human. Fortunately, he hadn't been allowed much time to brood on it.

"The only other human to undergo a body-part replacement that radical was Mick Taylor, your former best friend and partner. He went mad—I hardly need to remind you of that either, I warrant."

"No."

"You are unique, Steele. Something in your psychological makeup has enabled you to endure what no other can. I mean to find out just what that something is."

"Does this mean you're going to put me back in the coyote?"

"Indeed not, Lieutenant. Permit me to introduce you to the hidden wonders of *virtual reality*."

_18_

Donovan Steele was burning alive.

Through a dancing curtain of flame he could see Dr. James standing nearby, immaculate in his brilliant white suit.

"Some people would call this testing to destruction, Lt. Steele," he said with a smile. "Technically, that is correct. I abhor euphemism, however. I prefer to think of it as torture."

Steele's biceps bulged as he fought the manacles that held his hands behind the rough wooden post, already charred from use. "I thought . . . you said . . . it . . . *wasn't personal*," he managed to say, through the pain of the flames that were devouring his legs.

Dr. James's laugh was as dry as the kindling piled among the bundles of wood around Steele's feet. "Science is my life, Lieutenant. You might say it all comes to the same thing, really."

Something crackled beneath his feet. A new sheet of fire rushed up red before his eyes, and for a moment all there was was the pain. He had been on fire before, in that Midtown warehouse, but it hadn't been like this. Then he had traumatic shock to anesthetize him, and a final bitter clawing struggle for life to take his mind off the pain.

Now . . . he could feel his meat burn. He could feel his skin curl and crisp away, feel the tendons of his legs shrink and snap, their ends curling up, each alight. The fire was devouring his belly now like a starving beast, and the small amount of fat in his body ran like bacon grease in scorching rivulets down his legs. His fingers were burning like candles. . . .

He looked around once before the flames blistered his eyes closed. The fire surrounded him now in a continuum of pain. But through the shifting red he could see Dr. James, slim and white, and beside him now another figure, slight, oval, face framed by a cloud of long dark hair. . . .

Even a man like Donovan Steele had to scream then. *Had to*. And then there was only the screaming, and the burning, and the pain, on and on everlastingly, until. . . .

Cool. It was blessedly cool in here. Donovan Steele flung himself on the smooth, irregular cavern floor and sucked the coolness in through his skin.

After a time he rolled over and sat up. He raised his fingers before his eyes. In the dim jittering light they looked intact. He ran them over his face. Unblistered, whole, unburned. It had been a dream, somehow. The most vivid and horrible and realistic nightmare he'd ever known.

Torches guttered in sconces hammered into the melted-looking stone walls. He felt a tingling in his scrotum at the sight of fire. But the fire was small, tame, contained; it gave light rather than pain.

A rumbling sound. Vibration came up through the stone cavern floor, tickling his tailbone. Noise surrounded him. Fine dust drifted down in front of his eyes and fell on his nose.

He looked up. Impossibly, the stalactite-hung ceiling was descending toward him. The stone icicles were coming down to pin him to the floor.

Wildly he looked around. *What's happening? Is this another dream?*

He saw a hole opening in the floor three meters away. It was absolutely black, the black of a hole that led down into the earth and never came up again. He stared at it.

The stony tip of a stalactite pressed down on top of his head, gouging his scalp.

"You were thinking it was all a dream, weren't you, Lieutenant?" Dr. James's voice asked from somewhere. "It isn't. It's as real as anything in your life, in its way."

The implacably descending stalactites were pressing into his neck and shoulders now, forcing him down. "One way out, Lieutenant Steele. Better take it. Or will you disappoint me by simply lying down and allowing the stalactites to pierce your body?"

He made a clucking sound. "So passive, Lieutenant. I thought surely you were the sort to fight to the end, given any chance at all. In our introductory scenario you were given no chance at all. Here you have one. Best take it, Lieutenant."

On hands and knees, Steele tried to resist. The stalactites bore down, their points driving deep into his skin, stretching it to the breaking point. His arms bowed, and he collapsed to the floor. The welcome coolness of the hard stone had turned clammy, like a dead frog's skin.

He crawled across the floor on his belly. At the lip of the hole he paused.

What's down there?

Scraping and rumbling, the ceiling descended. No chance even to turn around and try to go in feet first. Steele extended his arms and slid into the hole.

From behind came an awful splintering, grinding noise as the ceiling smashed the stalactites into the cavern floor.

The hole did not lead to a straight vertical drop, as he had feared. It led down at a steep angle. He felt the first stirrings of panic awaken like bats in his chest. He was trapped, hanging head down into infinite night. The walls of the tunnel seemed to press in on him, growing tighter with every breath.

He began to slither downward. He had never been claustrophobic before. But now he felt the weight of the entire earth pressing in on him, and the blackness seemed to suck even the memory of light from him.

Calm down, he told himself. Whatever in the Devil's name was happening to him, he wouldn't escape from it if he flipped out. That smug devil James was right: he *wouldn't* give up.

The tunnel leveled out, then began to slant upward. It was definitely narrower now. The only way he could move his broad shoulders through it was to stretch his arms straight out in front of him. He was moving mainly by pushing with his feet and pulling with his fingers.

He stopped. He was exhausted. *Maybe there's something to be said for being a fusion-powered cyborg, after all.*

He wondered where he was. He wondered *what* he was. He

sure wasn't the coyote again. He tried enhanced night vision: nothing. Well, if there was no light coming into the tunnel no amount of enhanced light-gathering ability would help. He tried to cut his infrared vision in, to the same effect. Well, perhaps the walls of the tunnel ahead were of uniform temperature—which was cold; he felt the heat being leeched gradually from him.

He tried to turn on his sighting and range-finding lasers to light the way. Nothing. It was true. He was plain old Donovan Steele again.

He grinned. Somehow he'd achieved his goal: he was whole again, was real again, was human again. Now all he had to do was get out of here. . . .

A gurgling behind and below. He tried to look back, but his chest filled the tunnel. He could hear and smell the sudden swirl of water in the tunnel behind, could feel it splash against the soles of the light athletic shoes he seemed to be wearing.

In a heartbeat the water was up around his ankles. The fear of drowning seized him now. He began to force himself upward as fast as he could go.

The tunnel began to twist. He caught himself in a turning, screamed in terror, managed to push free as the water surged around his ankles. The tunnel was constricting again, growing tighter, threatening to trap him, hold him, crush him, let the water swallow him up.

Another bend, and light fell onto his face. It hit with an impact like molten silver, abrupt and painful, a disk of sunlight ahead and above. *Sunlight!* He was almost free.

He drove upward. And stuck. The stone walls narrowed, holding and trapping his shoulders in an intractable bond.

"No! *Noooo!*" The water was rising quickly now, it was about his knees. He scrabbled with his toes, desperate, stretched forth his arm as if he could extrude himself through the narrow point like toothpaste from a tube, reaching with his fingers as if he could grab the tantalizing sunlight and use it to pull himself to safety.

His fingertips felt the kiss of the sun. An enormous weight slammed down over the hole, shutting out the light, the world.

Donovan Steele gave a despairing cry. The dead stone weight threw it back in his face. The water came up around him and filled his nose and mouth and being, and the cold and the darkness seized him and bore him *down*—

He sat up with a start. It was dark in the bedroom he shared with his wife Janice. He and the sheets were soaking wet. He'd had the nightmare to end all nightmares.

For a moment he sat there with the sheet pooled around his waist, covering his face with his hands, breathing heavily. *What a dream!* What a series of dreams—like nothing he'd experienced in his life. It seemed as if the nightmare had gone on forever, and at the end it had grown impossibly horrible, impossibly strange.

He wanted a cigarette. He should go back to sleep. Tomorrow it was back into the scum pit of Manhattan's no-man's-land. Hardass Hardesty had yanked him off training detail— or was that part of the dream too, just wishful thinking? He shrugged, chuckled soundlessly.

A pleasant recollection of making love to his wife earlier in the night bubbled to the surface of his mind. He felt the slight tension on his cock where their mingled fluids had dried. Suddenly he wanted her again. In the dream he had lost her, lost everything. He wanted desperately to join with her, to hug her and cherish her and never let her go—and if tomorrow Captain Jacob Hardesty told him to report to Federal Plaza for a special assignment, he was going to tell him to shove the job up his fat ass and walk right out the door—

He rolled Janice over. But it wasn't Janice. It was his daughter Cory, her fourteen-year-old face painted in a garish mockery of a whore, her eyes staring blindly past him from bottomless pools of mascara and paint.

He jumped to his knees. The sheet fluttered away. His daughter's throat had been cut. She wore a cut-out bra and crotchless panties. The cutting hadn't stopped with her throat. Or maybe it had, but if so it had been going on a while.

Sour vomit filled his mouth. Horrible memories filled his brain. He looked down at himself.

Blood. It was blood that soaked the sheets, not sweat. He was covered with blood. It matted down the hairs of his chest and thighs and soaked the bush at the base of his cock.

Something snapped inside him. He tangled blood-dripping hands in his hair, threw back his head, and screamed at the ceiling: "James! *James, you motherfucker!*"

19

Misericordia bounced in her swivel chair and clapped her hands. "See? See, I told you he'd figure it out!"

Dr. James sat a moment longer, staring at the screen. It showed Steele kneeling on his bed beside the violated body of his daughter, who in the real world had died in his arms, shot down by accident years before in a firefight between the police and Stalker. Droplets of sweat, almost microscopic, stood out in a glistening line along the doctor's receding hairline.

"It took him long enough," he said at last.

He pressed a button. The screen went blank. Inside the IPU the counterfeit world dissolved around Donovan Steele.

Dr. James stood up. "Very well. That's enough for today."

In the intervals between torments, Steele floated in a strange nothingness. He shut out his audio/visual inputs and simply existed, detached from time and space.

He could see the attraction it held for Matrix. Even without the horror of Dr. James's hellish scenarios to contrast to, drifting in Void offered a very seductive lure: peace, to a man who'd known little of it.

Still, the Nirvana trip wasn't for Steele, even as the physical world failed to suit his brother. He came to suspect that the "testing" sessions were all that were keeping him sane. At least when he wasn't actually in them.

He put in a lot of downtime—or at least what he judged to be a lot, since the IPU had no timekeeping function he could call up—trying to figure out a way to escape. It didn't take many attempts to realize that, even if Dr. James hadn't taken such elaborate safeguards to keep Matrix captive, Steele would not have been able to emulate his brother. Whatever accident, whatever undocumented hardware feature or glitch in the transcription of the original Steele personality had given Matrix the ability to rove free in an electronic/information environment, Steele hadn't gotten it.

He was completely at the mercy of Dr. James. That knowledge created more pain than anything he experienced in any of the scenarios.

After the initial series, the scenarios turned more into elaborate torture tests than mere torture. Steele was compelled to perform tasks and solve puzzles under stressful and generally painful conditions.

He had to remove colored, sharp-pointed glass rods from a rack and rearrange them in a separate rack according to instructions on a display on the wall. The room was so chilly his breath was visible, and he was naked. Lights flashed constantly in different colors, making it difficult to tell whether his numbed fingers were fumbling out the proper rod or not, and when he made a mistake an electric charge blasted into his scrotum. Eventually he smashed the rods in frustration and froze to death.

He had to walk a cable above a floor of surgical-steel spikes. When he was halfway across the cable grew red hot. That was easy; he beat it by running the rest of the way and throwing himself onto the far side in a flying leap. Of course, the surface promptly tilted and dropped him onto the spikes. By that point, anything else would have been anticlimactic.

He tried again and again to tell himself that it was a dream, it wasn't happening. But it *felt* real. And when toothed wheels were grinding him to pulp from the feet up, it was impossible not to feel the same sick horror as if the mutilation were truly happening.

As bad as anything was the knowledge that the only reason he got respites of any kind was that his tormentors grew tired or bored. He was the perfect torture subject: he could never pass out, he could never find the prisoner's ultimate refuge in death. They could cut his fingers off, then his toes, then his feet and hands and so on, working until he was nothing more than a noseless, eyeless, earless, limbless head and torso. And then in the next scenario he would have his pieces back again in pristine condition for further abuse.

One session he ran a combat course. He was heavily armed; the obstacles were dangerous: flame and gunfire and pits of punji stakes and other traps. There were enemies, too: beautiful children armed with everything from spiked clubs to flamethrowers. He killed them with a fierce joy. They called him daddy as they died.

At the last he had to cross a minefield under sporadic gunfire before an airstrike covered the field with napalm. Huge-eyed children popped from spider holes to snipe at him or simply clutch at his legs with childish fervor. He ground his spiked boots into their adorable little faces and slogged on through muddy, fresh-turned earth.

He beat the clock by a fraction of a second, fell full length on the ground sobbing for breath. Behind him a jet whistled past, and a napalm hell erupted, orange and black, so close the soles of his boots began to melt.

He climbed to his feet. Misericordia stood there waiting with a smile. She was naked.

"You've done well, Donovan," she said. "I'm your reward."

"Are you another illusion?"

She shook her head. Her eyes glowed a blue like the sky. "It's a machine Dr. James has. It reads the electrical impulses of my brain, and induces sensations by means of a magnetic field. This world is as real to me as it is to you. *You're* as real as I am—outside."

She tipped her head back, baring her throat. Her breasts rode high on her ribcage. Her long hair fell down her back.

"Take me, Donovan Steele. I want you. Make love to me."

He turned and walked into the wall of flame.

It was a dining hall, echoingly huge and high. The walls were cream-colored with discreet green trefoil figures. Artificial candle flames glowed in wrought-iron sconces in the dark wood wainscoting. Real flames flickered at the tips of tapers set by threes in candelabra carefully spaced along the immense length of the table.

At one end of the table Dr. James sat eating steamed vegetables. At the other Misericordia ate a whole barbecued chicken, holding it with both hands. She ate ravenously, tearing at the bird with her sharp teeth like a hungry animal. Her face was orange with sauce.

Dr. James glanced up. "Really, Misericordia, I wish you'd eat more decorously."

A series of pops echoed in the dining hall, echoes chasing each other up to the ceiling, invisible in the darkness above. Then came a grinding sound, like continents rubbing elbows. Neither diner paid it any mind. It was just the volcano.

"I'm hungry all the time," the woman said sulkily. "*You* should know that. And if you wanted decorum, you should have given me the genes for it, shouldn't you?"

"You were an experiment, Misericordia. An early run; a rough draft, so to speak."

She set the chicken down on the tablecloth. The sauce stained the immaculate linen like orange blood. "What do you mean? I'm perfect!"

"Not really. An optimum specimen should be less contrary— should probably be entirely devoid of emotion, now that I think of it. A messy thing, emotion, and you know I can't abide mess."

He set his fork carefully down, picked up his napkin, scrupulously cleaned his lips. "There are physical flaws as well. Ideally, you might have more muscle mass. Your need to eat every two hours—quite a design flaw; you should be able to go for days without food and water. Your nose is too snubbed and those freckles—"

"I *like* my freckles! All my lovers say they're adorable."

"The ones who survive. Sheer sentimentality, in any event. They are irregularities, simple melanin deposits, and signs of imperfection."

She picked her chicken up, threw it down hard, and turned sideways in her chair. "You're just saying that to make me mad."

"Excessive temper. That's another trait to be avoided."

He sipped spring water carried down from the mountains west of the volcano from a cut-crystal glass. "Why are you

so obsessed with Steele?" he asked, setting down the goblet.
"You beat him decisively, after all. What further attraction can
he hold?"

"He's still the best," she said, pouting like a little girl.

Dr. James raised an eyebrow at her.

"Other than me. But I'm different. There's something about
him, a toughness, a strength, that no one else has."

She smiled impishly from behind a fall of hair. "You know
it too. That's why you're spending all your time concocting
scenarios to run him through. *You're* the one who's obsessed
with him."

"Ridiculous. I am merely intent on studying a unique subject
as comprehensively as possible."

She laughed at him. "You never pay any attention to me any
more. And I know why. You can't break him, and it *pisses
you off*."

He wadded his napkin and threw it on the table. "Really,
you act like a horrid schoolgirl. How can you claim to be a
pinnacle of evolution when you behave in such a way?"

"Spank me," she said, her voice low and smooth as honeyed
wine. "Wash my mouth out with soap. Do *anything*. I'm yours
to command, Doctor. I can give you pleasure—"

The door opened. She jumped to her feet. "Dammit, can't
we even *eat* in peace?"

Tapcis came in, screwing up his taupe face as if he'd just
stepped in dogshit. Or rather, as if he suspected Misericordia
had.

"I have important business with the doctor," he said, "and
none at all with his lab rat."

Misericordia picked up the chicken, flipped it in the air. As
it tumbled back toward the tablecloth she whirled a spinning
back kick into it. The chicken exploded.

"Don't start with me, Tapcis," she purred. "Or I'll be happy
to finish."

Tapcis had gone grayer than usual. "Stop this nonsense at
once," Dr. James said without heat. "What is it, Tapcis?"

"We have a potential loss of integrity in Adit F on Level 23. There's been a good deal of activity in the volcano
the last week. We've already lost the gym on that level,
and as you know Adit F runs south, directly beneath the
flow—"

"I know the structural details of my own stronghold, yes, Major."

"What's it got to do with you, anyway?" Misericordia asked. She took a protein bar out of the pocket of her jeans and unwrapped it. "You're security, not engineering." She threw the wrapper on the floor.

"If it's of concern to the doctor, it's of concern to me," Tapcis said. "I'm responsible for everything that goes on in this facility."

Dr. James pushed back his chair and stood. "Very well. I suppose we have to expect this sort of thing from time to time. I'll come and have a look."

"What about me?" Misericordia wailed. "Don't you ever have any time for me any more?"

Dr. James waved his hand at her without looking and left. Pausing long enough to show her a triumphant smirk, Tapcis followed.

_20_

The apartment door exploded inward in a shower of cheap plastic fragments. Young Donovan Steele looked up from his macroeconomics homework, instinctively ready to leap for the illegal pistol his father kept in the drawer of his desk. Urban kids got those reflexes.

What came through the door stopped him with his blood congealing in his veins. It was a mass of pus and blood and running sores. *A Screamer!* he thought. Some poor soul infected with Virus-3, far gone in lethal madness, infecting anyone he or she touched with the same horrible sickness.

But beneath the blood and boils was his mother's face.

"My children! My children!" she shrieked, staring madly around.

"Mom?" Donovan's ten-year-old brother Jimmy stood in the bedroom door, holding a model of an assault hovercraft in his hands. He stared at her as if suspecting she were dressed up for some kind of masquerade.

"My baby!" She grabbed Jimmy, crushed him to her chest, kissing him as if he'd been lost for days. He looked past her at his brother, eyes wide and mystified.

He screamed. Blood gushed from his bitten throat, sprayed his mother's face and the walls of the apartment.

She threw him aside. He lay moaning, trying to staunch the bleeding. She looked around the room. For a moment her distended eyes locked with those of Donovan, who was sitting transfixed with horror.

Instead she leapt on his other brother, six-year-old Michael. Their father came rushing in from the kitchen. "Dear God! *Elaine!*"

Michael was screaming and kicking. Steele's mother raised her head and stared at his father. A strip of Michael's skin hung from her lips.

Steele's father lunged for her, pulled her off. She sank her teeth in his arm like a weasel. He yelled, raised a fist, hesitated, then slugged her in the side of the head.

Nothing happened.

Donovan stood up. He should do something, anything. But he couldn't. He didn't know *what* to do. There was nothing to do, nothing right anyway. Down inside his brain he knew he had lived this before. But the helplessness and shame laid him open to the bone: *Oh, God, can't I do* anything?

His father shook off his mother, grabbed the chair beside the desk. Donovan knew what happened next: he managed to stun her, and then. . . .

Cat-quick, she ducked under the blow. The chair smashed the coffee table. She threw herself against her husband then, and the two of them crashed into the desk. Donovan heard his father's skull hit the corner with a sickening thud.

His mother raised her head and looked at him. She smiled.

"Come here, Donnie," she crooned. "Come here, mommy's precious angel. Mommy wants to give 'um *hug*."

No! This can't be! I've been through this before! It was all going wrong. He had to do something. There was only one thing *to* do, and he couldn't—

She started to stalk toward him. She held her dripping arms out to him. "Lullabye, and goodnight, time for *baby* to sleep," she sang.

He lunged for the desk. He tore the drawer open, grabbed the pistol. His mother came across the desktop. He leapt back, felt the wind of passage as her clawed fingers slashed an inch in front of his nose.

She rolled over on her back and blew a kiss from her bloody mouth. "You know your mommy loves you, Donnie."

"I love you, too, Mom," he said, and shot her between the eyes.

Moving as if all his joints had frozen, he walked around the desk. His brothers were infected. His dad too. Within hours the virus would be expressing itself, driving them into a psychopathic ecstasy of pain.

Holding the handgun in both hands, as his father had taught him, he carefully shot Jimmy and Michael, once each through the head. Then, almost blinded by tears, he swung the pistol toward his father.

The elder Steele lay on his side breathing in short gasps. He opened his eyes and looked up at his son.

"Donovan," he said, and swallowed. "Donovan, what are you doing?"

"What I have to," Steele sobbed. "You've always taught me to do what I have to. It's the greatest gift you ever gave me." And he shot his father, right above the bridge of his nose—

Emptiness. There was a lot to be said for it. *Especially* after a session like the last one.

He was shaken by how much James knew about him. There was nothing the man would not do, no memory he would not violate. He knew precisely what to do to turn Donovan Steele inside out.

But at least he was safe here, in the dark. For a little while he could know peace and—

And Jilly Romero sprang up before him, nude, her hands tied with barbed wire behind her back. A metal fence post had been shoved up her rectum and out through her mouth. A sign written in blood had been nailed to her left breast. It read THE WAGES OF SIN IS DEATH.

"*James!*" Steele screamed. "James, you bastard! I'll make you pay for this, before God I swear I will!"

Laughter echoed through the dream world, and then he felt himself shift again, back into the comforting void of the IPU.

He thought. *But I can't know for sure, can I?* It was the final refinement of torture: the violation of his sanctuary.

He had only two refuges remaining. Madness. And death.

He was in a clearing on a hillside, overlooking a valley. He was dressed for hiking: jeans, boots, plaid shirt. There were pine trees all around, but the undergrowth looked odd, strangely delicate. Wherever it was, it wasn't the Jemez Mountains. There was a crater in the valley beyond, but the birds were singing, and there was no hint of volcanic taint to the brisk air.

"Do you like it?" a voice asked. "I borrowed it from some old book I was reading because I liked the sex scenes."

He turned. She was on top of some boulders, squatting. She wore jeans and a man's work shirt with the tails tied up to bare her midriff.

"Sex and murder seem to be the only things that interest you," he said.

She hopped lightly down. "And eating. I do a lot of that. I need about ten times the calories you do, but it has its rewards."

She stood beside him. He started to draw away, stopped.

"What difference does it make?" he asked aloud. "You're not real, anyway. Just another figment of one of James's twisted dreams."

"No. I'm real. I told you before. There's a device that projects me into the scenario. I'm living this just as you are, in real time."

He frowned, shrugged. He didn't see what difference it made one way or another.

"Okay. I'll take your word for the reality part." He looked at her. "The rest of what I say still stands."

Her face went white. For a moment he thought she was going to attack him.

She shook herself, walked a few steps away, hugging herself beneath her breasts. "Maybe you're right. But I'm not a figment he plays with much any more. *You're* his favorite toy now."

"Am I supposed to feel sorry for you?"

She turned around. "Look. I'm not here trying to seduce you, all right? I'm here because I want—I just want to talk to you. That's all."

"Never talked to anyone for very long before you killed them, eh?"

She threw up her hands and turned away. "I'm what I was made. I don't know anything different." A pause. "I'm lonely."

The wind blew her long hair. Birds sang. He wondered what would happen if he took three quick steps and grabbed her by the neck. She was off her guard now—maybe he could snap her neck before even she could react. He wasn't sure what good it would do, but it would probably make him feel better. . . .

"Do it," she said. He stiffened. "No, I can't read your mind. But I could hear from the way your feet moved on the pine needles that you tensed, could smell the stress in your sweat . . . go ahead. Break my neck. I won't stop you. I'll come back and let you kill me again and again, if you'll just *talk* to me."

"And if I kill you," he asked, "will that be real?"

She turned. "As real as it was for you each time. I've watched you die a hundred times, Donovan. Each time you were brave."

He sat down. He felt . . . he didn't know what he felt.

After a moment she came and sat near him, almost close enough to touch, but not quite.

"What's James got up his sleeve this time?" he asked. "What's going to spring out and eat my face?"

"Nothing. The doctor has nothing to do with it. He's off inspecting someplace where the lava's in danger of breaking in." She giggled. "He'd be mad if he knew I was here. So mad he might actually do something to me, treat me like a naughty little girl. Treat me as if I'm *real*. You can't know what it's like to be treated as—as some kind of artifact."

He laughed. "Yes, I can."

"Yes. I guess you can." She got up on her knees facing him. "You still don't believe me, do you? Here—"

She waved a hand. In midair an image appeared of her sitting alone in the room on the far side of the partition from the IPU, a headset obscuring her eyes and the upper half of her face. "See? No Dr. James anywhere in sight."

"How do I know that's real?"

"You don't. How are you going to know anything's real, ever again?"

He took a deep breath. "I don't know. That sounds more like one of Matrix's lines. How is he?"

"Fidgeting. He hates having a body." The image winked out.

"How did you do that, anyway? Bring that picture of you into the dream world, or wherever we are."

"This is an interactive program. It responds to your actions, right? You just have to know how to *massage* it—"

She was suddenly a great red dragon, looming over him, fire jetting from her nostrils, wings outspread. He jumped to his feet. *I knew it. It was all a trick.* Talons like black scimitars reached for him—

Misericordia's fingers closed lightly on his chin, cool and dry. She tipped his face down, stood on tiptoe, kissed him lightly on the lips.

"You see?" she said. "Anything's possible if you just know how."

She danced away, arms outstretched, pirouetting with her face turned toward the analog sun. She went faster and faster, until she collapsed laughing on the short grass.

He came and sat down next to her. Eventually she rolled over onto her belly.

"I want to have a child," she said.

He looked at her.

"Dr. James says I can't. He says I'm infertile. I wasn't *designed* to have kids. I was designed to kill. But I think I'd rather have a baby than anything in the world."

She looked at him. "Tough luck, huh? No sympathy for the human killing machine . . . even from another killing machine?"

He laughed. It was a genuine laugh, if mostly bitter. "You got me there. I have to admit, ah—"

"Miseri. That's my nickname."

"Miseri. Right. Ah—Miseri, I have to admit there are times when you seem more human than others."

She shrugged. "I am—"

"What they made you. Yeah. I heard."

"Except I don't know if that's really true. It's something I say. But I wonder if you're ever really anything but what you make yourself. I mean, when they replaced most of your body, when they replaced your brain and poured it full of your memories and God knows how many other people's did they *make* you? Were you only what they made you?"

"I thought so. For a while, anyway."

She shook her head. "I don't think so. I think you were

Donovan Steele before, and Donovan Steele after. I think that's why Dr. James hates you, why he's so obsessed with breaking you no matter how long it takes. Because you're untouchable, incorruptible, something he can't control. That drives him crazy, not being able to control—"

She broke off, turned her head away, said, "Huh? What—?" to someone Steele couldn't see.

She vanished.

He stared. Slowly the mountainside began to fade.

"Just what in the *hell* do you think you're doing, Tapcis?" Misericordia raged. She tore the headset he had removed from her head away from him. She hoped he'd fight for it; pulling off one of his fingers would feel very nice about now.

He surrendered it with an oily smirk. "Dr. James's orders. You're not to be allowed to use the equipment in here. I can't tell you how sorry I am."

"Who's going to stop me?" she flared. She knew that his men could take her—if there were enough of them, battle-armored and heavily armed. She was almost mad enough just to see.

But he didn't rise to the challenge with his customary anger. "Why, Dr. James's orders will, of course," he said. "Or aren't you obeying him any more?"

She whirled and marched out of the room.

21

He waded thigh-deep through reeking black muck. The sword in his hand was nicked and dull from hacking his way through loathsome, misshapen foes. But at last he was in sight of the Gates to Dawn, the way out, to freedom and rest.

The thick black filth began to bubble before him. It humped up into a mound, cascaded off the back of a vast squat toad-shaped beast rising from its hiding place.

A forked tongue snaked out, plucked the sword from his fingers before he could react, threw it away. Globular eyes fixed on him.

"I am Tsathoggua," the creature said in an earthquake voice. "I shall crush your bones for their marrow and suck your eyeballs from your head, little man."

Donovan Steele drew himself up to his full height and remembered words spoken in a meadow no more or less real than this foul swamp.

"I don't *think* so," he said. "I think I deserve to get out of here after all I've been through. And when I don't get what I deserve, I get *mad*. You know what anger feels like to me, you ugly fat toad thing? I'll tell you: When I get really and truly mad, it makes my hair stand up. It's like static electricity."

He held up a hand, squeezed it into a fist. Squeezed until blue sparks came shooting out between his fingers. The smell of ozone cut through the sewage reek like a blowtorch flame.

He held up his fist. Reflected blue lightning danced in the toad-thing's gelatinous eyes.

"And when I get *really, really* mad," Steele said, "I like to *hit* something."

He strode forward and punched the toad-monster in the nose. It squealed like a goosed steam engine as a fat blue spark seared the tip of its nose. It tried to rear its bloated bulk. Sizzling blue energy enveloped the creature, consuming it. It fell onto its back with a mighty thrashing, kicking up huge waves of black crud. Then it lay still.

Steele dusted his hands against each other. "And you know what? I feel *better*."

His fingers arched on the console as if he were playing a piano recital, Dr. James stared at the screen. "What happened?" he demanded.

He turned around and glared at the technicians in their pastel jumpsuits. "Can anyone tell me how that was possible? It wasn't in the script I prepared, I can promise you that."

The techs all looked at each other as if hoping consensus would hit on a scapegoat in a hurry. "Maybe it was just a glitch in the software," one said.

"Yes, that's it," another said. "Undocumented feature."

"Software as complex as these scenarios is bound to display occasional chaotic features," a third said happily.

Dr. James glared around at them in silent fury. He understood group dynamics as well as the next man.

"Very well," he said in a soft voice. "But it had best not happen too often; I *hate* chaos."

He turned back to the board. Standing neglected off to the side, Misericordia smiled and munched her protein bar.

With a squeal, the pulley played out another ten inches of cable before jerking to a stop again. Dangling from the cable by his wrists, Steele grimaced at the jolt of pain.

He looked down at the vat of clear liquid seeming to spin slowly a foot below his feet. "An acid bath," he said. "That's supposed to terrify me. It does. In fact, it makes my blood run cold. So cold that I could freeze to death."

Ice crystals began to form in his hair and eyebrows. A wind

rose, howling, chilling as if it blew from between the stars, surrounding him with a whirlwind of ice shards.

Out of sight above a capstan turned, playing out a final foot of cable. Steele's booted feet hit the surface of the acid bath with a thump.

The acid was frozen solid.

Steele flexed his lats. Brittle with cold, the cable that bound his wrists snapped. Pieces of it fell tinkling to the acid ice.

Steele massaged his wrists and grinned.

The dogs were on him. They had hunted him through a maze of featureless cubes. Now they had brought him to bay.

They surrounded him, leaping and snapping. These were no ordinary dogs. They were robots, shiny silver metal, and their teeth were hypodermics filled with a hideous toxin. One bite and you died in lingering agony.

Steele turned around. "I'm tired of this. I'm tired of *you*. Dry up and blow away."

He swept his arm outward. The dogs blew away like scraps of paper in a spring New York breeze. Their fangs broke with musical chiming tinkles as they bounced off the giant cubes.

"Are you getting the *idea* here, Dr. James? I'm not a help-less puppet any more. The string done broke. I'm not Matrix, but this is my world now. If you want me, you're going to have to come in after me *yourself*."

The exercise cycle made a rhythmic cicada noise. Dr. James maintained his body with the same scrupulous care with which he maintained his laboratory instruments. And approximately the same degree of affection.

Misericordia eased the two-hundred-kilogram barbell into its rack and jumped up off the pressing bench. She didn't need exercise to maintain her strength and muscle tone, but she had felt like getting the kinks out of her shoulder blades. A little light workout was just the thing.

Whir, whir, whir, the cycle said. "I'm shutting him off," Dr. James said.

Misericordia paused with her head tilted, unbraiding her hair. "What?" she said.

"Your friend Steele," Dr. James said, his pale legs pumping joylessly away at the pedals. "He's showing signs of being able to do what Matrix did. He's too dangerous. And anyway, I'm through with him."

"You're what? He—he didn't break, did he?"

Dr. James shook his head. "No. It's only a matter of time, of course, but I've invested enough of that already."

"Well, why do you want to get rid of him? What are you going to do with all those clones you had grown from the Download tissue samples?"

He smiled thinly. "Use them, of course. I've been deluding myself, focusing on Steele's *character*. It's really a mystical concept, if you think about it. Not scientifically verifiable, not scientifically interesting.

"No, the important thing is his abilities. I'll download those into the clone bodies by themselves, without his personality. Without anybody's personality, for that matter."

"But wait," Misericordia said. "What about Steele's ability to retain downloaded information?"

"If the abilities begin to fade, I shall simply download more clones."

"What if—what if it drives them crazy?"

"That's the very best thing about it." He leaned forward as the difficulty of pedaling increased to mimic climbing a hill. "These Steele clones will have no will at all, except of course for mine. If they go mad, it doesn't really matter. As long as they continue to function—and if they don't, they can be replaced."

"I thought it was important to you to find out just what made Steele different," she persisted.

He stopped exerting effort, let his legs freewheel to a stop. "What I found out is that it doesn't really matter. All Steele is that's of any consequence is muscularskeletal fitness, experience, and muscle memory. The rest is supernumerary, and best expunged."

He looked at her. "Why so insistent, my child?"

"Your work—"

"Means nothing to you. You've become infatuated with him, haven't you?"

"I—no. That's the silliest thing I've ever heard."

Dr. James swung a leg off his bike, settled to the thin gray-blue carpet of the gym floor. "All the more reason to have an end to our Lieutenant Steele," he said. "Anything that interferes with your loyalty to me likewise interferes with your reason for existence."

He bent to pick up a jump rope. She stamped her foot. "Damn it, I *am* loyal to you. I *love* you. You *made* me!"

"Love," he said, beginning to skip rope. "Tsk, tsk. Don't use words whose meanings you don't know. It leads to sloppy thinking, and that can be fatal to someone in your line of work."

She started to speak, raised her hands, dropped them, and stormed out of the gym. Dr. James shook his head and devoted his attention to his workout.

A few more turns of the rope, and here came Tapcis, drifting among the Nautilus machines like a blue and khaki cloud.

"You seem thoughtful, Dr. James."

"Do I?" He was puffing, but only slightly. He kept himself fit. "It's Misericordia. She's growing progressively more spoiled and willful, almost as if she thinks she's a real girl, and not a construct."

"Imagine," Tapcis said. "The impertinence."

"It's not that. She is becoming difficult to control." He shook his head. "That could greatly complicate matters. *Greatly.* Sometimes I'm almost sorry I made her."

Tapcis's eyes shone. "It's my job to simplify your life whenever possible, Director. I think of it as my mission in life."

Dr. James glanced sideways at him. "Do you, now? Excellent. I'm glad that *one* person near me has some sense of proportion."

He stopped skipping, let the rope fall. Tapcis caught it before it hit the carpet and hung it on a peg.

Dr. James started toward the door. "Oh, by the way," he said over his shoulder. "I want Matrix terminated before tomorrow. See to it, won't you?"

"Your wish," Tapcis breathed, "is my command."

Misericordia was just sitting down to her bowl of chili when the alarm sounded. "Damn!" she exclaimed. It was the third time she'd tried to settle down to eat, and the third time she'd been interrupted.

She didn't just get irritable on an empty stomach. She *needed to eat*. Her optimized metabolism required immense amounts of fuel; much more than twenty-four hours without food would kill her. Perhaps, as Dr. James said, it was a design flaw. She didn't see how it could be avoided, herself, unless she'd been created to drag around twenty or thirty kilos of body fat as backup, and that would slow her way down.

It had been over three hours since she last ate, and the hunger pangs were every bit as painful as the bullet Rob Honesty had put through her belly, already half-forgotten.

But the alarm was singing its insistent song, and she had her duty. She pushed away from the table, giving her chili a last regretful look. She could nuke it when she got back, at least eat it hot.

"All right. I'm coming." She stood up and ran out of the commissary.

Leaning against the wall, Major Thurman Tapcis watched the humanoid—as he thought of her—burst out of the commissary, turn away from him, and run off up the hall to the nearest guard station. She gave no sign of having noticed him.

He smiled wetly. Even the *creature*, with her wild-animal senses, could overlook his presence. He had that effect on a lot of people. He enjoyed being overlooked—as long as Dr. James noticed him, and acknowledged him.

Dr. James had been overlooking him recently. Since *she* emerged from the forced-growth chambers. That would change, soon.

A nod is as good as a wink to a blind horse, Tapcis's grandmother always used to say. He knew his master's mind.

Better sometimes than Dr. James himself did.

Half an hour later Misericordia returned grumbling. Another rabbit kicking dirt on a motion sensor—if it was even that much. This was one of those nights when everybody on watch got twitchy, it seemed.

Lucky I was on the lookout for Steele, she thought. As slack and dull witted as Tapcis's men were, chances were one of them would've gotten tired of false alarms and cut his sensors off line in just the sector Steele picked to infiltrate through.

It wasn't lucky for Steele, though. Thinking of him gave her a funny disoriented sensation in the pit of her stomach. She wished he didn't have to die. Of all the people in the world, he seemed the most likely to understand who she was and what. Not to love, necessarily, though that would be good. Not even to *like*. Just understand.

She was too ravenous to bother reheating her chili in the microwave. She grabbed the bowl and started shoveling it into her mouth before she even sat down. She was getting weak-kneed from hunger, and her head was light.

She had slammed three spoonfuls down her throat when she noticed her tongue was burning. Though her sense of taste was more than humanly sensitive, like all her other senses, she sometimes enjoyed eating extremely spicy food as exquisite self-torture. But this wasn't hot chili, except perhaps to the Texans who canned it for export; it just had mild red powder for seasoning.

And even jalapeños or red Indonesian paste never had this effect on her. Her tongue burned savagely, as if she'd bathed it in acid. It was actually swelling in her mouth.

The pain hit her in the stomach then. This was worse than Honesty's bullet, far worse. It was like a bomb going off inside her.

And now she smelled what haste and desperate hunger had masked before: the acrid stink of the lye with which her food had been laced.

22

Misericordia staggered backward out the commissary door and fell against the corridor's far wall. Her mouth was red and swollen. A line of fire ran from it to her stomach.

Someone had been very, very clever. With her metabolism, Misericordia needed plenty of not just food but air. When ingested, a caustic agent like lye causes massive internal swelling and bleeding.

The bleeding was no trouble; she knew her healing system could contain it and repair the tissue damage the lye had done, no matter how painful. But she would choke to death long before that happened.

She reeled half-blind down the corridor. Already taking in air was difficult, like trying to breathe through thick blankets. A pair of techs turned the corner, headed for the commissary and a coffee break. They saw her inflamed face and pain-crazed eyes and fled.

She came to a restroom and fell inside against the metal door of a utility closet. She felt for the knob. It was locked, of course. In other circumstances she might have laughed at that: Who in a top-secret facility would want to steal mops and drain cleaner?

She wasn't exactly in a humorous mood. She buckled the

door next to the lock with three quick punches and pulled it open.

The light came on. She could barely tell. She was getting almost no air now, on the ragged edge of a blackout. She gasped at a fresh stab of pain, sagged against the doorjamb. Her eyes darted frantically, searching the racks and shelves. It was a thin chance, but it was all she had.

There—in the plastic tub at the back. She grabbed a half-meter length of white polymer pipe, about two centimeters in circumference. She tipped her head back.

She rammed the pipe down her throat.

Her gag reflex caught it, briefly held it. She exhaled explosively to open her epiglottis, forced the pipe down with both hands. She could feel the tortured tissue tearing. That didn't matter. It would heal, if she lived.

To live, she must have air. She drove the pipe ruthlessly in, probed until she found where her trachea branched from the esophagus. Air whistled through the pipe. Ignoring the pain, she pushed a final time, sealing it.

Deliberately she lay down on her side on the hard, cold tile floor. The pain was intense, unbelievable. She pulled herself into a fetal ball to wait for her body to defeat the poison.

Matrix sat in full lotus on the thin carpet of his apartment/cell. He was trying to levitate.

On his wanderings through the world's digitized knowledge, he had read that back in the twentieth century, before people got generally too busy for that sort of thing, a famous Indian mystic went around claiming that he could teach people to levitate. He even claimed that if everyone in the world studied levitation, the world's conflicts would cease.

He was probably right about that last one, Matrix thought; they'd be too busy trying to will themselves up off the carpet, just as he was. For the rest of it, though, he had his doubts. For one thing, no impartial observer had ever caught the great man in midair, unless he was seated next to him on an Indian Air Lines 747. Photographs of the mystic in flight were reputed to exist—none had made their way into the data banks—but they had all been taken by devoted followers, who might be suspected to've been willing to overlook little details like trampolines or suspension from the overhead fixtures.

Still, Matrix was trying to levitate. As he saw it, he had a hell of a better claim to being a mystic entity than any twentieth century Third Worlder dressed in a bedsheet. Matrix, after all, had more or less called himself into being. The great man had a mother and father; Matrix had mass-storage devices. The great man claimed descent from a Godhead; Matrix descended from a read head and a write head. The great man claimed to be seeking to transcend being. Matrix had been there, done that. He *had* traveled along common household electrical wiring, no trick photography involved.

In short, he figured if *anybody* was going to levitate, he was the man to do it. Besides, he had nothing better to do. They weren't even letting him talk to his brother.

His eyes were closed. He concentrated like hell. No sign of positive buoyancy.

Maybe I should take up astral projection, he thought. *I've kind of done that already, come to think of it. If I could get back in the wiring, I could spring Don, and we could blow this malt shop. . . .*

The door opened. He didn't deign to look around.

Bulky gauntleted hands caught him under the armpits, pulled him to his feet. "All right, gramps. Nap time's over."

A couple of jocks in security battledress flanked him. Their bulletproof visors were raised, their faces young and arrogant. *Gramps?* he thought. *Does Don get treated like this?*

"Show some respect, junior," he said, trying to shake their hands off. "This body may look to be in its forties, but it's a lot younger than you are. Don't pay too much attention to the model year."

"Yeah, yeah." They kept a firm hold on him and started to walk him in a semicircle to point him at the door.

"Where exactly are you gentlemen taking me?"

They glanced at each other. *Uh-oh*, he thought.

"You got an appointment," said the one on his left.

A hand came and tapped the grinning kid on the shoulder. He frowned, turned his head around.

Matrix saw a flesh-toned blur streak in the front of the helmet, and a lot of blood come spraying out. There was a sound like a dropped watermelon.

The guard fell. The other gaped. "What the fuck, over?"

A small pale hand came around the side of his helmet. The

fingers sank literally *into* his cheek, blood welling abruptly as
a shout around them. Before the scream of pain could burst
out of him, they snapped his head around with a loud crack.

Matrix looked from the two twitching, cooling bodies at
his feet to Misericordia. Her mouth and cheeks were red and
swollen, as if she had mumps.

She knelt to wipe her dripping hands on one's uniform
trousers. "They were coming to kill you," she whispered. Her
voice sounded like a county road after a cloudburst.

"I got that impression. What are *you* doing?"

She stood up and handed him the first guard's sidearm,
butt first. He stared at it in shock, accepted it. It was a
replica Desert Eagle .44 Magnum, just like Donovan Steele
used to carry.

"What am I supposed to do with this?"

He pressed the muzzle between her breasts. Her eyes met
his. "If you want to kill me, go ahead. But your brother
dies."

He let the barrel tip back until it pointed at the fluorescents
overhead. "You *do* know how to use one of these?" she
asked.

"You forget who I am."

"You're the one who turned his back on this plane of being."
She jerked her chin at a dead guard. "That one's about your
size. Better put on his armor; there's going to be lots of lead
flying soon."

Level Seventeen was maximum security, even within the
super-secret LANL complex. It was where the director kept
his pet labs. The young woman marching with wrists bound
before her and puffy lips pressed tight in front of a bulky
dark-visored security man had been born on this level.

Technicians pressed back hastily to the walls when they
passed. Some of them watched with surprise as Dr. James's
life work walked by in restraints.

Others watched in relief.

Three technicians were hard at work in the observation room
next to the IPU, taking last-minute readings. Between Matrix's
two-year sojourn in the bottle and Steele's much briefer stay
there would be data to last them all for several lifetimes.

The door hissed open. Misericordia walked in, followed by a security guard whose large frame was made larger by his battle armor. Her wrists were wrapped in nylon restraints.

The shift boss was standing by the door with one hand raised to scratch his bald head and a notebook comp in the other. His eyebrows rose in comic surprise.

"Ms. Misericordia, what are you doing here? You're not supposed to be—"

Strain showed briefly on her face. The nylon restraint popped. So did the chief tech's eyes.

Following current Strike Force vogue—they were the trend setters for cops and security types worldwide—Lab Security men customarily wore two sidearms, one in a belt holster, the other under one arm. Her arms free, Miseri turned, pulled the 9mm out of her escort's shoulder rig, pivoted, and shot the tech through the open mouth.

The other two whirled from their boards. One stood up holding his hands out before him. "Wait! No problem, no problem—"

Misericordia shot them both.

The .44 Magnum from his belt holster in hand, Matrix stared at the smear of blood the tech had left down the armored glass divider. "Did you really have to—"

"I'm not in the mood," she said, stabbing her fingers at the control boards. "Get those two bodies out of the corridor before somebody notices, will you?"

Matrix reholstered his weapon and went out the door, preventing it from closing with one booted foot. He came back in dragging a pair of guards by the collars of their battle dress. One had the handle of an issue belt knife jutting out from the bottom of his visor. The other's head lolled bonelessly.

Matrix let the door slide shut. "I don't see how we were able to walk in here so easily."

"My retinas will open any door in this place," Miseri said. "That bastard Tapcis hasn't gotten around to changing that."

She pressed a final button. Two lines of molecular bonds in the partition that defined a door-shaped section were severed by an electrical impulse. The door retracted into a side wall.

Misericordia ran to the Download unit, a thing like an outsized dental chair on casters, which was parked by the wall of the observation room. "Give me a hand here. There's not much time."

"Why are you doing this, anyway?" Matrix asked, helping her maneuver the chair through the opening.

"Let's just say I'm ready for a change of scenery."

"You mean you've had a belly full of the good Dr. James?"

They stopped the chair next to the IPU. She looked at him across it.

"I've had a *mouthful* of that bastard Tapcis, let's say," she slurred. "I'd never do anything to hurt Dr. James, not directly."

"Helping us escape is going to give him a pain."

She smiled. "Fine. Think of it as an attention-getting device. Now take off the helmet and sit down in the chair."

He hesitated. "What's the matter? Don't you want your brother freed? There's no time to prep another clone. Tapcis's men are going to come pouring through the door at any minute."

He glanced up at the gleaming cylinder of the IPU. "Yes. Yes, I do. Even if it means going back in there to stay. Walking around free out here means a lot more to him than me."

"That's not necessary," she said.

He looked at her.

She licked her lips with a still-swollen tongue. "There is another way. But it, uh . . . it'll still demand a *bit* of sacrifice."

He frowned at her, not comprehending. Evasiveness was definitely not her style, in conversation, anyway.

Then he put back his head and laughed.

23

The first thing Donovan Steele was aware of was gentle pressure on his lips.

He opened his eyes. Misericordia's face was gazing into his. "I awaken thee with a kiss," she breathed. Her voice was more throaty than usual, rougher somehow.

He caught her by the throat. She grinned at him. "Think very carefully before you act," she said. "It could be a habit you'd like to get into."

"I doubt it." He frowned, took a deep breath.

A look of wonder spread over his face. He touched it with his fingers, breathed on them, tasted them, ran them over the arms of the massive white chair.

"It's real," he said.

"What gave you your first clue?"

"It's too—too complete, somehow." He looked down at himself. "Why am I in battle armor?"

"Because you're going to need it."

"Is this another test?"

"You can think of it that way if you want. But if you pass this one—freedom."

"I don't believe you."

She shrugged and turned away. He caught her by the wrist. She turned back.

"Why are you doing this?" he asked.

"Look, maybe it's time for you to get back in the habit of acting before thinking. Or at least asking questions. We're running out of time here."

Effortlessly she broke his grip. "And keep this in mind: you aren't a one-man army anymore. You don't have fusion power and lasers and a nysteel skeleton. You're just plain, old Donovan Steele."

She laughed at his look of amazement, kissed him lightly on the cheek.

"I am," he said. "*I am*."

He drew the replica Desert Eagle from the belt holster, made sure it was on safe, twirled it, stuck it back in its holster. "Kids, don't try this at home," he muttered. "The hero used to do that in my favorite old movie back when I was a kid."

He looked at her and grinned. "What you meant to say is, I'm *still* Donovan Steele," he said. "Let's go."

Two technicians in lime-green jumpsuits were in the instrument-lined room, one sitting with her feet up reading a magazine, the other pouring coffee into a lab beaker. Misericordia pointed her finger at them.

"Leave," she said. They left.

"You're mellowing," Donovan Steele said. "You didn't kill them."

She shrugged and pushed open the inside door.

He sniffed, frowned. "Where are we, a kennel? What are we doing here? I thought we were in a big hurry. And where's Matrix? I came for him, I'm not leaving without him."

He followed her through. It was a kennel, with two rows of wire cages stacked one atop the other. In the nearest a very familiar-seeming coyote got to his feet and regarded them with yellow eyes.

"Boy, am I glad to see you two," the coyote said.

"You mean, all the time I was in that coyote body, I could *talk?*" Donovan Steele demanded, shifting his grip on the American-made 30mm automatic grenade launcher Misericordia had scrounged for him. They were in a lift, headed down. The volcano surrounded them with a sizzling sound, like frying fat.

"You never tried," the coyote said smugly. "You're not the inquisitive type."

"I didn't have anybody to talk to," Steele said. "I was all by myself in some nature preserve a few klicks away. You must have a speech synthesizer like the one Jilly fitted me with, when I was a skeleton."

"You're not as dumb as you look, Donovan."

Steele frowned. "They must have some kind of tracking transmitter built into that body, plus a remote-control means of knocking you out. When they wanted to transfer me to the bottle, it was just, bang! One moment I was trotting along with my tail held high, the next you and James and Misericordia were peering in at me. We'd better be careful they don't do the same to you."

"Remember that equipment I smashed back at the kennel?" Misericordia asked. Along with a slung assault rifle she wore a backpack she'd brought out of a guards' ready room. None of the occupants would be needing its contents any more, whatever they were. "You thought that was just vandalism, didn't you."

The LCD floor counter read 23. The door slid open. Beyond lay darkness. Steele had the sense of an expanse of emptiness, but could make out no detail. He grinned; there was something to be said for being a cyborg with a super-enhanced sensory package. Although his stolen Strike Force-style armor gave him a variety of enhancements, they were less efficient and convenient than what he was used to.

Yellow polymer tape crisscrossed the door. A sign on a sandwich stand said:

LEVEL CLOSED

DANGER

TOXIC GASES

Matrix sniffed and yipped. "Aside from that toxic gas, what's down here?" he asked.

"A way out," Misericordia said, "if the lava doesn't seal it. But nobody lives forever, right? Okay, Steele, you've got an air sampler in that helmet. You can call it up with a voice command."

"Got it." He shut his visor, hit the switch with his chin and said, "Air test."

A microwatt laser wrote a list of contaminant levels by parts-per-million in blue on the inside of his visor. Sulfur dioxide and carbon monoxide were high.

"Air breathability marginal," a voice said in his helmet. The words were echoed on his visor display. "Recommend exposure not exceed fifteen minutes."

"This shouldn't take that long," Misericordia said. "Steele, you got high right."

He nodded. She popped the tape and ducked out.

Steele stepped forward. The darkness was virtually complete. The only ambient light was what spilled from the elevator's open door. He moved quickly right, launcher ready, to avoid being silhouetted against it.

He called up thermal imaging. There was a greenish glow from what seemed to be the far side of a large room.

"Heat from the lava intrusion," Misericordia said behind his right ear. She had a portable communicator with a mike patch taped to her throat and a bone-conduction speaker on her mastoid process. "That's the way we're heading. The adit starts about fifty meters farther down."

"Great." He'd had enough of lava to last him a lifetime. In fact, it *had* lasted him a lifetime. It was just that his life had been brief after he encountered the stuff on an intimate basis.

He felt something brush his shins. "Just me," Matrix said. He had a communicator like Miseri's jacked directly into the base of his skull. His tail and ears were high.

"I still can't see jack," Steele said. "I'm going to active IR."

"Go for it," Misericordia said.

"Infrared, setting one, illuminate now," he said. A helmet-mounted spot kicked in.

It was a big room, at least three stories high and very wide. IR gave poor detail, but the impression he caught as he swept the beam around was that it was unfinished, not yet partitioned into labs, offices, or dorms.

"Expansion space," Miseri said. "Room to grow into. Dr. James has great plans for the lab."

"Not world domination?" Steele asked.

"Sure. Aided by an army of invincible Donovan Steele clones. Isn't that what everybody wants, world domination?"

"I want as little to do with this world as possible," Matrix said, "although being a coyote does have its intriguing side."

"I'll settle for us getting out of here intact," Steele growled.

For the moment it seemed to be used as informal storage—without Dr. James's knowledge, Steele guessed. There were crates and boxes stacked by the walls, and equipment of unidentifiable type and purpose stood around the floor, covered with plastic against the ever-present volcanic dust.

"Do we go for speed or go for caution?" he asked.

"I don't think the alarm's been given yet," Misericordia said. "The clock's sure not on our side."

"Right. We go for it. I'll lead—"

"*I'll* lead off," Matrix said. "Smaller target."

They moved out. Matrix trotted ahead and slightly to the right, dodging between mysterious humped shapes. Misericordia followed trailing left. The only reason Steele knew where she was was that he could pick up the heat signature of her body and knew where to look. She had approximately the same heat signature as a normal human. Apparently her tough skin was a good enough insulator to cut down the heat emissions of her hyperactive metabolism.

The green glow was coming from the southwest corner of the oversized room. The elevator had let them out in the middle of the east wall.

Exaltation sang in Steele's veins like a drug. *Freedom!* He thought he'd never leave the lab alive. Now the way out lay just around the corner. . . .

They had worked their way a third of the way across the floor. Steele saw the odd polygonal blob that was Matrix stop.

"I smell something," Matrix said.

"I do too," Misericordia said.

Steele crouched. He hit the chin switch. "Illumination off," he said. "Go to maximum gain."

His visor went red. Faint blotches of yellow were visible, clustering in clumps on the western wall.

The room exploded in blinding light.

24

"Freeze!" Major Thurman Tapcis's voice detonated from giant amplifiers, terrible and commanding. *"Put your weapons down. We don't want to hurt you. Dr. James has special plans for all of you."*

At least, that was how he had it worked out in his mind. As it worked out in reality, he had just said, *"Fr—"* when his quarry scattered in all directions.

"Shoot! Shoot them all down!" Tapcis's angry scream echoed through the vast room.

Steele had ducked behind a plastic-sheeted shape four meters long and sternum high when a hurricane of fire broke from the west wall of the room. He hoped whatever it was he was hiding behind was bulletproof. As he knew from agonizing experience, not even the best armor was, not totally.

Tapcis had set up huge banks of halogen lights in the corridors that gaped like rows of mouths from the west wall. Obviously he was hoping to blind his quarry and freeze them to the spot. Like jacklighting deer.

Steele was protected. His visor was opaqued; the thermographic image of the room he'd been looking at was another laser-painted projection. If Miseri had been caught looking into the lights, however, her supersensitive eyes might have been burned out.

"Visual spectrum, step down one," he ordered his helmet. "Is anybody blinded?" He heard bullets thunking into polyceram housing and bouncing from metal to ricochet screaming away. Whatever he was hiding behind was reasonably solid, at least.

"I wasn't looking up," Matrix reported. "I don't need to rely on sight anyway. This body's ears and nose tell me all I need to know."

"I'm dazzled," Misericordia said. "But I'll get over it. My pupil-contraction time is fast. And I don't necessarily need to see, either. Wait one."

He glanced back toward where he gathered she had gone to ground. Her hands appeared above a low, sheeted form, holding her assault rifle upside down. The gun spat a burst.

It was a shooting technique Steele was familiar with: unseasoned troops, such as non-Strike Force cops and fledgling gang members, used it a lot. Though to call it a *technique* was probably overstating. It was firing blind, plain and simple, and the main effect it generally had was to give the shooter a wholly unwarranted sense of accomplishing something. Steele was surprised to see Misericordia employing it. But cat-and-mouse games were her specialty, after all. Maybe she couldn't handle a stand-up firefight—

A series of loud popping sounds, and the glare in the big room diminished. She had shot out a bank of floodlights.

"Muscle memory," she explained over the comm net. The rifle appeared, snarled again. A second bank blew.

"Cover me," she said. "Time to move."

A little grudgingly, he admitted to himself that once again the woman knew what she was doing. Every weapon in line of sight was busy chewing at the machinery she was hidden behind. At least one automatic grenade launcher was firing. Fortunately its 30mm rounds were dropping long.

He came to one knee and fired a burst of HE from the shoulder. Explosions walked along the far wall at the second-story level. A third set of spots exploded.

He dropped. Hitting the lights had been fortuitous. He had mainly been shooting to take the heat off Miseri while she shifted cover and to get a look around.

"I'm clear," he heard her say. "I'll take the second level lights. You take the third. You handle that?"

"Yes."

This time she fired three quick bursts. Steele bobbed up in time to see three light banks go. *She really is good*, he thought.

He didn't want to be outdone. Four light banks still glared from the top level. He started walking shots left to right, double tapping them, firing a two-shot burst from the slow-cycling launcher at each light.

A bullet struck his visor. Sparks seemed to shoot from the bones of his neck as his head torqued left, and he went sprawling.

Bullets spattered like rain on the cement floor on all sides of him. He rolled desperately back into the lee of the shrouded machine.

"Sloppy," Misericordia said. "Missed one. Better move."

Oh. Resentful and a little embarrassed that she'd had to point the obvious out to him, he jumped up and ran crouching for another solid-looking bulk. Bullets plucked at his armored vest as he sprinted across five meters of open floor. As he dove for his new hiding place, a launched grenade burst shattered the cover he'd just left.

He heard the last light bank on the third level blow. It was getting dark in here; there were only two lights remaining, both at ground level.

"You want the grenade man?" Matrix asked. "I got him locked; these ears are *great*. Get ready for voice input."

"Go."

Matrix recited coordinates, which were accepted by the AI in Steele's armor and routed to the fire-control routines. Steele pushed back a meter or so from the object he was hiding behind and angled his head up. A little box appeared, an aimpoint to drop a burst indirectly on the spot Matrix had pinpointed. He hunted a little left and up. The box brightened and began to blink.

"Left and right magazines, two-and-one mix. Three rounds, fire now."

Unlike Janet Virág's prized FN, which had a single drum magazine, Steele's Remington-made GI model had two half-moon magazines, one on each side of the bullpup receiver.

Because the grenades were caseless, the propellant held in an epoxy matrix bonded to the rear of the stubby olive projectiles, the receiver could feed from either side; there was no need for an ejection port. By means of switches on the weapon, or the battle-dress' integral fire-control system, you could even mix and match.

The fire-control routines tripped the launcher's electronic initiator. Three grenades chuffed away.

Steele was instantly up and moving, determined not to commit the mistake the enemy launcher operator had. Bullets cracked past his head. He threw himself flat.

"Right on the money," Matrix said.

Steele heard screaming. He had fired one HE and two white phosphorus rounds. Battle armor was terrific stuff, but WP was its very great weakness. The phosphorus flakes ate right through, and unless you could shrug out of the bulky armor in time, you burned.

"Where do we go now?" Steele asked, listening to gunfire snapping over his head. "I've got to admit, I'm fresh out of ideas. I don't think we can go right through these boys."

"There's a small door that leads out to the north," Misericordia said. "Lay down smoke to cover us, and we'll break for it."

"Done. Matrix, go." Steele let the rest of the WP half-moon box go on manual, dropping short bursts just shy of the wall. That was how a weapon as ugly as white phosphorus came to be "legal" under international law: it was carried on the books as a smoke round, though everyone knew better. In truth it did produce a lot of very dense white smoke, though it tended to form vertical tentacles instead of a nice solid wall. Still, if there was no wind—as in here—it laid a decent screen.

And when they saw those white starfishes reaching out their arms right in front of their positions, the security boys felt a strong urge to keep their heads *down*.

Fires blazed up as the echoes of the grenade bursts died. The polymer sheeting was non-flammable, as was most of what it covered, but if there was a way for something to burn, WP had a way of finding it. Dodging among shadows, Steele held back from further fire. Most of the enemy's lights were down, the room was full of smoke, and the fires were going to play hell with their IR vision. He didn't want to make things easy by giving them a nice fat muzzle blast to track on.

Misericordia slipped through the door ahead of him. She hadn't fired either. Matrix raced up next, only to drop his butt and skid. He bumped his nose on the metal door, stifled a yip.

"Forgot you didn't have hands, huh?" Steele said. He yanked open the door.

"I was just getting used to *having* them."

Steele followed himself inside. The corridor was lit by the soft glow of ceiling panels. Why the corridor was lit and the room outside was not Steele had no clue.

Misericordia was leaning with her back against the wall with her rucksack and rifle propped beside her, breathing deep and laughing.

"Don't you think you were a little hard on the kid about shooting at the lights?" Matrix asked her. "Three out of four taken out is pretty good, under the circumstances."

"It was *excellent*. I was only kidding. Who do you think taught me everything I know?"

She hugged Steele, laid her head on his chest. He felt a strong stirring of attraction for her. She was really strikingly beautiful.

So's a king cobra. He pulled away.

"We're heading in the wrong direction," he said.

"No worries," Miseri said. Her voice was less husky than it had been, and the redness of her mouth had subsided. She turned around. "Give me a hand up, big fella?"

Steele slung his launcher, grabbed her around the waist with both hands. She flexed her knees, pushed off like a ballerina. He grunted in surprised effort, flexed his shoulders, then lifted her, held her up while she undid the toggles on a broad louvered vent cover overhead.

She dropped back to the floor and grinned at Steele. "You forgot how much I weigh."

"I also forgot I'm not a super cyborg anymore," he admitted ruefully.

"You and Matrix go ahead," she said.

Steele hoisted Matrix up into the open vent, jumped, caught the lip, chinned his way in after him. Misericordia boosted herself up and began rummaging in her backpack.

"Move down the vent to the first cross passage and wait for me," she said.

The passage wasn't totally dark. Light bled through from side vents. Steele looked at Matrix, shrugged. Matrix trotted ahead. Steele followed on hands and knees, his grenade launcher slung beneath his belly.

She came up to them in a moment. "Let me past. I know where we're going."

She rubbed her body along Steele's like a cat as she slithered past. "What'd you do back there?" he asked.

"Left a Claymore in the duct with a trembler trigger and reclosed the vent," she said. "If they figure out where we went and try to follow—" His ambient-light enhancement caught her smile.

"What about the backblast? If they come through before we're clear—"

She smiled. "We'd better hurry, huh?"

She was elevated, almost giddy, with spots of color glowing high on her cheeks. Obviously the added element of danger was getting her off.

It occurred to Steele that he was trusting his life—and Matrix's—to the hands of the deadliest enemy he'd ever faced. He didn't see what other way they could play it. At the moment, the greatest danger seemed to lie in the fact that she regarded this all as a great game.

She led off. Matrix, unarmed except for his sharp teeth, came next. Steele brought up the rear.

They moved quickly, pausing for a quick check down each cross passage before passing it. Steele felt his eyes begin to water, and his throat felt as if it had been sandpapered.

"Getting hot in here," Matrix remarked.

"We've had several breakthroughs on this level. They're probably going to have to just fill a lot of the western sector with cement as a buffer."

By way of emphasis the volcano rumbled like a giant's dyspeptic stomach. Steele and Matrix traded looks.

They came to another junction. "We go right here," Misericordia said. "We're going to try to flank them."

They turned and began to head south. A sharp crack sounded. Steele tensed with his hands braced on the walls of the vent shaft, suddenly convinced that the lava was about to break in on top of them. Then he felt a sudden shove of rolling overpressure from behind.

"Claymore?" Matrix asked over his furry shoulder.

Steele nodded. "They finally figured out which way we went."

Misericordia giggled with delight.

Moving rapidly they came to a T-passage. Right led back toward the ambush. Left, to the west of them, the passageway was closed by a cave-in.

"End of the line," Misericordia said. "We're almost out."

"If Tapcis doesn't have his whole force waiting for us in this adit," Matrix said.

She shook her head. A lock of hair had pulled free from her braid and fallen across her nose. She blew it away.

"Tapcis's instinct is going to be to cover his ass. Once his ambush failed, you can bet he had almost everybody he's got running around trying to track us down. He's going to be afraid we'll just pull out and try to break out somewhere else."

"If you say so," Matrix said dubiously.

Misericordia grinned. "You have a better idea, pup?"

He cocked his head, ears at full extension. "No. They're in the shaft now too. We need to get out of here."

Steele leaned over the grille. The corridor beneath was dimly lit, like the one they'd entered the ventilation system from. Suddenly he felt blind and deaf. The sensory-enhancement package of his battledress was laughably inferior to what he'd had as a cyborg.

"Nobody below," he subvocalized. "Is there anybody nearby?"

"Not immediately," Miseri replied the same way. "Walls are too thick to pick up heat from anybody who's not right under us."

"Too much noise from the lava to hear anything in this direction," Matrix said. "Those toxic gases the sign talked about aren't making it easy to smell, either."

Steele looked at Misericordia. "Nobody lives forever, right?"

"We sure won't just sitting here." She reached for the louvered grate, pulled. With a small skreaking noise it buckled. She lifted it out and slid it quietly aside.

Steele lowered himself through the hole. He dropped, got his hands on his grenade launcher as his rubber bootsoles hit the cement floor. Five meters down the corridor to the east was a doorway with darkness beyond. The west end of the corridor was closed by a metal door. Four doors were set in the north wall. The south side was blank.

"Clear for now," he said. "Move."

Matrix landed on Steele's head, scrambled down his back. Steele grunted, stayed in a ready crouch, ready to fire in either direction as Matrix scuttled west and pressed himself up against the first door.

"Misericordia?" he asked.

Her bare feet and jeans-encased legs appeared through the hole. She dropped to the cement with barely a sound despite her surprising weight.

"Left another Claymore on a trembler for the boys coming from behind."

"They'll see this one."

"Then they'll be thinking about it, not us."

She ran to the first door, popped it off its hinges with a blow from her elbow. "C'mere and cover me."

Steele did, hunkering down half inside the door. He concentrated on the western door, unsure what might be lying behind it.

Misericordia darted down the corridor. She had just passed the next door when she spun and dived back toward it, screaming, "*Behind you!*"

Ruby glare, a shattering crack, and the smell of burning flesh filled the passage.

25

Misericordia screamed in agony. She crashed through the side door. Steele pivoted. The open doorway to the east was crowded with Lab Security troops in battle armor. He fired a burst.

Launched grenades don't explode until they've traveled a certain distance, to protect the shooter. Steele was within the minimum distance of the closest man, who wore a bulky backpack and was trying to swivel the weapon he held at the hip to bear on Steele. The burst of HE grenades would not punch through his body armor, but knocked him into the men behind. Three went down in a heap.

Misericordia came skidding out the door she'd disappeared through on her side, firing full-auto at leg level. Lab Security armor protection, like most police-style body armor, ended at the crotch. Men screamed and fell, clutching shattered shins and spurting thighs.

With the doorway somewhat cleared, Steele straightened. He brought the launcher to his shoulder, fired at a downward angle. The grenades hit the cement just on the far side of the door, behind and among the attackers. This burst barely had time to arm.

A moment and it was over except for the moaning of several bulkily armored, supine forms. Misericordia jumped up, limped back up the corridor. Smoke trailed from a black hole in the calf of her left jeans leg.

"Are you badly hit?" Steele asked.

"Oh, yeah. But I'm alive, babe, which means it'll heal."

"What the hell was *that*?" Matrix asked.

"Backpack laser," Steele said. He thought wistfully about the pop-up laser he'd had mounted in his arm as a cyborg. It hadn't survived the wreck of his verti in Tijeras Canyon.

The laser man had rolled over and was trying to get to his feet. Misericordia kicked him in the visor. His head snapped back a lot farther and faster than was good for him. Her wounded leg buckled and she sat down hard.

"What're you doing?" Steele demanded, trying to cover in both directions and expecting more bad guys to start dropping out of the ceiling vent at any moment.

"This could come in handy," she said, tugging the backpack free. Unless Steele missed his guess, it carried a portable fusion generator like the one he used to have in his belly. "Matrix, can you grab my pack? I can't carry both."

"Got it." He ran in the door she'd smashed through, emerged dragging the rucksack with the strap in his mouth.

He stopped. "Oops," he said. "Someone's at the door."

"Right," Steele said, and fired a burst of high explosive.

The door exploded outward. Somebody screamed. Steele saw figures staggering amid clouds of smoke and stirred-up volcanic dust, started to call for his weapon to load white phosphorus. *No, we've got to be in that corridor in about ten seconds*, he thought, and fired another burst of HE.

Miseri's recovered laser pulsed. Air rushed away from the beam's hot core, then collapsed back in with a thunder-like crash. The red shaft transfixed a man. Steam exploded from his chest and he fell.

The laser cracked twice more. Two more dropped. Steele held his launcher on the dust slowly settling in the doorway.

"Clear," Misericordia said. "Next up is the adit. They'll be waiting there."

A shot sounded behind. The Claymore Misericordia had left just inside the vent shaft blew. Steele heard the clatter of steel pellets rushing down the shaft, wondered if the pursuers had been smart enough to trigger the mine by firing blind around a corner.

"Company soon," he said. "Load WP. Four-round burst. Fire now." The four grenades thudded off back the way they'd come. The burning flecks and dense choking smoke would slow the pursuit a bit more.

Seconds counted. It was stiflingly hot here, and the gases were beginning to make Steele giddy. He called for HE and fired another burst through the shattered doorway to the west to shake up any defenders at the mouth of the adit.

They ran that way, Steele hugging the right wall, Misericordia and Matrix the left. When Steele chanced a glance around the doorframe, a snarl of automatic fire greeted him, and grit went flying from the wall by his head.

"Machine-gun!" he yelled, ducking back.

Miseri showed him her teeth. "Got it." She pivoted to her left, fired a pulse from the laser, swung back into cover as rifle fire crackled through the doorway.

Through the smoke behind them, shouts. Steele realized the enemy was about to risk a rush through the smoke and burning pellets. A bullet whanged off the doorframe centimeters above his helmeted head.

His eyes met Misericordia's. "Let's go." He came around in a crouch, let loose an HE burst west as she fired the laser.

Something gray and furry streaked between them. "Matrix, where are you *going?*"

"No time to waste!" his brother shouted to him. Gunfire crashed from the adit mouth. It was aimed too high to hit an animal running on all fours.

The machine gunner was lying with his head against the butt of his piece and a hole in the center of his visor. Misericordia's laser had flash-boiled the fluid in his brain. The steam had ruptured his skull, and brains were leaking onto the cement.

Another armored man was kneeling over him, trying to recover the machine-gun. Matrix left the ground. He hit the man, and both went flying.

As soon as coyote collided with man, Misericordia was racing after him, moving with astonishing speed. Steele scrambled after her, not sure what was going on, but knowing now was a good time for a little improvisation.

The corridor widened at the mouth of the adit, which was a curved opening. There were half a dozen men still functional there. Matrix leapt clear immediately of the man he had tumbled, sank his sharp teeth into another's calf. The man snapped his head around with a cry. Misericordia shot him through the neck.

Matrix jumped at another who was drawing a bead on the chest of the charging Donovan Steele. A coyote isn't really big enough or powerful enough to be a match for a man, but it can be a nuisance; Matrix grabbed the sling, dropped his haunches, and yanked the man off balance.

A guard standing by the north wall fired a burst from the hip. Miseri threw herself against the south wall to avoid it, and without checking her momentum caromed into him.

The man playing tug-of-war with Matrix saw Steele looming over him, and grabbed for the pistol in his shoulder holster. Steele buttstroked him with the grenade launcher. He went onto his back with his throat exposed. Matrix tore it out with his teeth.

Misericordia was hugging her man. He howled as she snapped his spine.

A guard faced Steele. He knocked the grenade launcher from Steele's hands with a blow of his M-27. Steele stepped into him, drove his fist into the pit of the man's stomach. The armor damped most of the blow but not all. The man doubled. Steele backed him into the wall, hit him twice more in the gut. Then he snapped the .44 from his shoulder holster, stuck its muzzle under the visor, and pulled the trigger.

Matrix was wrestling with the man he'd first sent flying. The last guard broke and ran down the adit. Misericordia recovered her laser rifle and shot him through the middle of the back. He ran two more steps, went to his knees and over onto his face.

"Matrix, look out!" Steele yelled. The coyote leaped nimbly aside. A slash of a fighting knife shaved hairs from his tail.

Steele shot the guard in the belly. The armor stopped the .44 Magnum round from penetrating, but the shot knocked the air out of the man. He dropped the knife and curled himself into a ball, gasping for breath.

Without remorse, Steele aimed for the exposed back of the man's neck between helmet and collar. He fired. The man straightened convulsively, blew bloody foam all over the cement, and lay still.

"Matrix," Misericordia called, "can you go get my ruck-sack? Hurry; it's hot in here."

Matrix dashed back for the last doorway. Steele holstered the .44, recovered his grenade launcher, and took quick stock of the situation. It *was* hot, so hot he could feel it through the soles of his boots. The heat seemed to radiate from the walls.

"Look there," Miseri said, gesturing down the corridor. A huge jack had been emplaced holding a thick two-meter square chunk of polyceram against the south wall of the adit. A large crack ran up and down from behind the patch. There was a mound of black stone at the base of the patch and spilling across the floor that Steele recognized with a shock as recently cooled lava.

"Here's our incipient breakthrough," Misericordia said. "When Matrix gets here, we'll make it *more* incipient."

A gunshot. Matrix came zigzagging into the mouth of the adit, making good time despite the weight of the backpack he was dragging. "They're coming," he said, as Misericordia tore open the pack.

"White phosphorus," Steele commanded, depressing the chin switch. He fired the rest of the half-moon magazine back up the corridor, snapped in his final box of WP and let it go too.

Misericordia peeled the facings from the sticky tape on hefty prepackaged charges of plastic explosive. She fastened one to the polyceram patch, right over the crack, and another on the jack.

"That ought to do it," she said, standing up. Steele saw the palms of her hands were blistered from contact with hot concrete and metal. "Even if it doesn't block the passage, it's going to discourage them."

She stood up, slung her rifle. "That's it. A hundred more meters and we come to a hatch that lets us out on the other side of the flow."

Scarcely able to believe it, Steele began to walk toward freedom. In his mind he paced it off: *sixty meters, fifty, forty.* . . . Misericordia was at his side. Despite himself, he hugged her.

A voice behind them cried, "*Misericordia!*"

Misericordia stopped, turned back. Slim and immaculate in its white suit, the figure of Dr. James emerged from the impenetrable white phosphorus smoke, hands clasped primly behind his back.

Misericordia seemed to shrink. "Shoot him, Misericordia," Steele said.

As if against her will she began to drift back toward her creator. "What do you want," she asked sullenly, fingering her laser's trigger switch.

"I want you to come back," Dr. James said.

The woman stiffened. "You had that man try to kill me."

"Sweetheart, I didn't know. He did it without permission."

"You're in my way, Misericordia," Steele said, low and urgent. "I can't get a shot—"

"What did you call me?"

Dr. James dropped his eyes. "I—we sometimes don't realize what we have until we've lost it. And yet—"

He looked at her, and his eyes were shining. "And yet I dare hope I haven't lost it yet. Haven't lost you yet. Misericordia, child, I love you."

"He's lying, Misericordia."

She was walking faster now. Steele started after her.

"Donovan, we're almost out," Matrix called after him. He ignored him.

"Daddy," she said. Her voice was the voice of a little girl. "Daddy, do you *really* love me?"

"Remember what she is, Donovan. We're so close—"

Dr. James picked his way around the jack. Behind him the smoke was beginning to dissipate into the poisonous air. Well back, the adit was packed with security troops.

"More than a daddy, my dear, my only love. I want you. You and only you."

"Miseri, *get out of the way*," Steele said.

She stopped and spread her arms slowly from the sides. "I love you, Daddy," she said. "Take me, Daddy."

Dr. James was a scant ten meters away. He smiled. "I shall."

His hand came from behind his back. In it was a stubby pistol. It made a loud cough, and a magenta flare streaked toward Misericordia's breastbone.

The flare was moving fast enough to penetrate deep into her chest cavity, and it burned almost as hot as white phosphorus. It would lodge in her heart, and burn, and burn, until her heart was too thoroughly cooked to function any more, despite her inhuman vitality and powers of healing. She made no move to dodge. She stood there awaiting the flare. Magenta light glittered in the tears in her smoke-blue eyes.

Matrix hit her calves from behind at a dead run. She tumbled over backward. The flare hissed harmlessly over her.

Donovan Steele sidestepped the burning lethal thing. He came into firing stance, knees slightly bent, weight forward, dropping his shoulder to pull his Desert Eagle and aim it in one smooth motion, just the way he'd taught so many Strike Force rookies. He shot Dr. James through the chest. A red blotch spoiled the white perfection of his waistcoat and he flew backward. Steele fired three more times before Dr. James hit the floor. Every one connected.

The security forces charged. Donovan Steele staggered back as bullets smashed into his armored torso. He saw the corridor light to a flash from Misericordia's laser rifle, and then a bullet hit him in the visor, snapping his chinstrap and knocking his helmet off his head.

Well, at least we tried. The Desert Eagle roared futile defiance in his hand.

With a double crack the charges blew. Lava surged into the adit, almost white and blinding in the smoke-charged dimness.

Guards screamed like damned souls as molten stone engulfed them.

Epilogue _____

Dawn was paling the sky to the east when they broke out of the stinking darkness.

For a moment they simply stood, a transhuman entity trapped—at least for the moment—in the body of an animal; a beautiful and amoral woman who was more and maybe less than human; and a man who felt tears of gratitude well up suddenly in his eyes that he was just that: a man.

Misericordia grabbed Donovan Steele's head and dragged his face to hers for a passionate kiss. For just a moment he responded. Then he put his hands over hers and pulled gently away.

"I'll never love you," he said. "I'm grateful for what you've done, for me and for my brother. I'll be your friend, I'll help you any way I can. But I won't love you."

She only laughed at him. "I'm Misericordia," she said, "and I always win."

The coyote trotted a few meters to the south, raised his head and howled at the dawn. "I've always kind of wanted to do that," he said, very self-satisfied. "Now, why don't we get the hell out of here?"

Donovan Steele glanced back at the bulk of Pajarito Plateau, rising black above the lava river. Then he started to move purposefully up the wooded slope. Misericordia wanted to hold his hand. He let her.

The first dawn birds were beginning to sing.

The human body is a wonderful machine. It can endure incredible damage and still function, still survive.

Over the years Dr. James had kept his body meticulously tuned. Now what was left of it clung tenaciously to a small thready pulse of life, in spite of the four huge bullet wounds in the body cavity, in spite of the lava that had burned off the legs at the hips and cooked the intestines.

Tears ran over Major Tapcis's smooth taupe cheeks. "There's no hope?" he cried. "No hope at all?"

The doctors exchanged nervous glances. The head of security for Los Alamos National Laboratories did not have a reputation for taking disappointment well. He did have a reputation for an almost unwholesome degree of devotion to his superior. He had put on a heat-resistant suit and slid across still-glowing lava on a thick slab of polyceram to rescue Dr. James in person.

No one wanted to tell him the heroic rescue had been wasted.

"Major," the chief of the surgical team said, "the Director's will to live is incredibly strong. But the enormous damage done—"

"But he can't die!"

"We can put him on life support," the surgeon said, "but it's only a matter of time. The regeneration techniques don't yet exist that could repair damage this severe."

The doctors stood then, and waited, hardly daring to breathe. They were convinced the major would order them shot on the spot.

Instead he smiled through his tears. "There is a way," he said.

Dr. James opened his eyes. "I don't feel right," he said. "What's going on?"

"You were . . . hurt," he heard Major Tapcis say from somewhere outside his field of vision. He shifted in the chair he found himself reclining in. "It took . . . extraordinary means to save you."

"What on earth are you talking about?"

Tapcis stepped around where the doctor could see him. "Here, Dr. James," he said, holding out a hand mirror. "See for yourself."

Frowning, Dr. James accepted the mirror. He looked into it.

Into the gray eyes of Donovan Steele.

He threw back his head and laughed.

IN A WORLD ENSLAVED,
THEY'RE FIGHTING BACK

Freedom is dead in the year 2030—megacorporations rule with a silicon fist, and the once-proud people of the United States are now little more than citizen-slaves. Only one group of men and women can restore freedom and give America back to the people:

THE NIGHT WHISTLERS

The second American Revolution
is about to begin

THE NIGHT WHISTLERS #1: by Dan Trevor
Available October 1991 from Jove Books!

Here is an exclusive preview . . .

Prologue

Los Angeles, 2030: Seen from afar, the skyline is not all that different from the way it was in earlier decades. True, the Wilshire corridor is stacked with tall buildings, and there are new forms in the downtown complex: the Mitsubishi Towers, a monstrous obelisk in black obsidian; the Bank of Hamburg Center, suggesting a vaguely gothic monolith; the Nippon Plaza with its "Oriental Only" dining room slowly revolving beneath hanging gardens; and, peaking above them all like a needle in the sky, the Trans Global Towers, housing the LAPD and their masters, Trans Global Security Systems, a publicly held corporation.

The most noticeable difference in this city is a silver serpentine arch snaking from downtown to Dodger Stadium and into the Valley, and in other directions—to Santa Monica, to San Bernardino, and to cities in the south. Yes, at long last, the monorail was constructed. The original underground Metro was abandoned soon after completion, the hierarchy claiming it earthquake prone, the historians claiming the power elite did not want an underground system of tunnels where people could not be seen, particularly since the subways in New York and other Eastern cities became hotbeds of resistance for a short period.

But to fully grasp the quality of life in this era, to really understand what it is like to live under the Corporate shadow, one ultimately has to step down from the towers and other heights. One has to go to the streets and join the rank and file.

Those not lucky enough to inherit executive positions usually live in company housing complexes—which are little more than tenements, depending upon the area. The quality of these establishments vary, generally determined by one's position on the Corporate ladder. All in all, however, they are grim—pitifully small, with thin walls and cheap appliances and furnishings. There are invariably, however, built-in televisions, most of them featuring seventy-two-inch screens and "Sensound." It is mandatory to view them during certain hours.

When not spouting propaganda, television is filled with mindless entertainment programming and endless streams of commercials exhorting the populace to "Buy! Buy! Buy!" For above all, this is a nation of consumers. Almost all products, poorly made and disposable, have built-in obsolescence. New lines are frequently introduced as "better" and "improved," even though the changes are generally useless and cosmetic. Waste disposal has therefore become one of the major problems and industries of this society. A certain amount of one's Corporate wages is expected to be spent on consumer goods. This is monitored by the Internal Revenue Service and used somewhat as a test of loyalty, an indicator of an individual's willingness to contribute to society.

The Corporations take care of their own on other levels as well. Employees are, of course, offered incentive bonuses, although these are eaten quickly by increased taxes. They are also supplied with recreational facilities, health care, and a host of psychiatric programs, including Corporate-sponsored mood drugs. In truth, however, the psychiatric programs are more feared than welcomed, for psychiatry has long given up the twentieth century pretence that it possessed any kind of workable technology to enlighten individuals. Instead, it baldly admits its purpose to bring about "adjustment"—the control and subjugation of individuals "who don't fit in."

Because this is essentially a postindustrial age, and most of the heavy industry has long been shifted abroad to what was once called the Third World, the majority of jobs are basically clerical. There are entire armies of pale-faced word processors, battalions of managers, and legions of attorneys. Entire city blocks are dedicated to data entry facilities, and on any given night, literally thousands of soft-white monitors can be seen glowing through the glass.

There are also, of course, still a few smaller concerns: tawdry bars, gambling dens, cheap hotels, independent though licensed brothels, and the odd shop filled with all the dusty junk that only the poor will buy. And, naturally, there has always been menial labor. Finally there are the elderly and the unemployed, all of whom live in little more than slums.

Although ostensibly anyone may rise through the ranks to an executive position, it is not that simple. As set up, the system invites corruption. Even those who manage to pass the extremely stringent entrance exams and psychiatric tests find it virtually impossible to move up without a final qualifying factor: a sponsor. Unless one is fortunate enough to have friends or relatives in high places, one might as well not even try. If there ever was a classed society, this is it.

In a sense then, the world of 2030 is almost medieval. The Consortium chief executive officers in all the major once-industrial nations rule their regions with as much authority as any feudal lord, and the hordes of clerks are as tied to their keyboards as any serf was ever tied to the land. What were once mounted knights are now Corporate security officers. What was once the omnipotent church is now the psychiatric establishment.

But lest anyone say there is no hope of salvation from this drudgery and entrapment, there are the national lotteries.

Corporately licensed and managed, the Great American Lottery is virtually a national passion. The multitude of ever-changing games are played with all the intensity and fervor of a life-and-death struggle, drawing more than one hundred million participants twice a week. There are systems of play that are as complex and arcane as any cabalistic theorem, and the selection of numbers has been elevated to a religious experience. Not that anyone ever seems to win. At least, not anyone that anyone knows. But at least there is still the dream of complete financial independence and relative freedom.

But if it is an impossible dream that keeps the populace alive, it is a nightmare that keeps them in line. Ever since the Great Upheaval, the Los Angeles Corporate Authority, and its enforcement arm, the LAPD (a Corporate division) have kept this city in an iron grip. And although the LAPD motto is still "To Protect and Serve," its master has changed and its methods are as brutal as those of any secret police. It is much the same in all cities, with all enforcement agencies around the world under the authority of Trans Global.

What with little or no legal restraint, suspects are routinely executed on the streets, or taken to the interrogation centers and tortured to or past the brink of insanity. Corporate spies are everywhere. Dissent is not tolerated.

And yet, in spite of the apparently feudal structure, it must be remembered that this is a high-tech world, one of laser-enhanced surveillance vehicles, sensitive listening devices, spectral imaging weapon systems, ultrasonic crowd control instruments, and voice-activated firing mechanisms.

Thus, even if one were inclined to create a little havoc with, for instance, a late-twentieth-century assault rifle, the disparity is simply too great. Yes, the Uzi may once have been a formidable weapon, but it is nothing compared to a Panasonic mini-missile rounding the corner to hone in on your pounding heartbeat.

Still, despite the suppression, despite the enormous disparity of firepower, despite of the odds, there are still a few—literally a handful—who are compelled to resist. This savage world of financial totalitarianism has not subdued them. Rather, if it has taught them anything at all, it is that freedom can only be bought with will and courage and blood.

This is the lesson they are trying to bring to the American people, this and an ancient dream that has always stirred the hearts of men.

The dream of freedom.

_1_

The city was still sleeping when the whistling began. The streets were still deserted, and the night winds still rattled through strewn garbage. Now and again, from deep within the tenement bowels came reverberations of harsh shouts, the slamming of a loosely hinged door. But otherwise there was nothing beyond the echo of that solitary whistler.

For a full thirty seconds Phillip Wimple stood stock-still and listened, the collar of his sad and shapeless raincoat turned up against the foul wind. He looked out at the city with calm brown eyes, his slightly lined face expressionless. He stood as detectives the world over stand, with all the weight on his heels, hands jammed into the pockets of his trousers, his cropped, gray head slightly cocked to the left.

Although not a particularly reflective man, those high nocturnal melodies had always left Wimple vaguely pensive. As to the fragment of some half-remembered tune that continually tugs at one's memory, he had always felt compelled to listen— to turn his tired eyes to the grimy Los Angeles skyline and allow the sounds to enter him.

A patrolman approached, a sleek doberman of a man in Hitachi body armor and a Remco mini-gun harness. Below, on a stretch of filthy pavement that skirted the weed-grown hill, stood four more uniformed patrolmen. Gillette M-90s rested on their hips. The darkened visors of crash helmets concealed their eyes. Turbo-charged Marauders idled softly beside them in the blackness.

"With all due respect, sir, the Chief Inspector wants to know what's holding us up."

Wimple turned again, shifting his gaze to the distant outline of an angular face behind a smoked Marauder windshield. "Well, tell her that if she would be so kind as to join me on this vantage point, I would be more than happy to explain the delay."

"Sir?"

"Ask Miss Strom to come up here."

Wimple returned his gaze to the skyline. Although the whistling had grown fainter, scattered by the predawn breeze, the melody was still audible: high and cold above the city's haze; dark and threatening in the pit of his stomach.

The woman entered his field of vision, an undeniably grim figure in black spandex and vinyl boots—a full-figured woman, about an inch taller than his five-ten. Her shimmering windbreaker was emblazoned with the Corporate logo: twin lightning bolts enclosed in a fist. When Wimple had first laid on eyes on her, he took her as a welcome change from the usual Corporate overlord. Not only was she smart, but she was beautiful . . . in a carnivorous way. He had also liked her fire, her determination, and her willingness to fight for a budget. But that was three days ago. Now, watching her stiffly approach through the smog-choked weeds and yellowed litter, he realized that Miss Erica Strom was no different from any of the boardroom commandants sent down to ensure that the Los Angeles Police Department toed the Corporate line.

"You want to tell me what's going on?" Miss Strom planted herself beside him.

Wimple shrugged, studying her profile: the chiseled features, the red-slashed lips, the hair like a black lacquered helmet. "Ever heard a rattler's hiss?" he asked.

Strom narrowed her sea-green eyes at him. "What are you talking about?"

Wimple extended his finger to the sky to indicate the echo of the unseen whistlers. "That," he said. "That sound."

Withdrawing a smokeless cigarette, one of the Surgeon General–Sanctioned brands that tasted like wet hay, Wimple said, "Think of it like this. We're the cavalry. They're the Indians. Maybe they can't touch us up here, but down there it's a whole different story."

"So what are you trying to tell me? That you want to call this patrol off? You want to turn around and go to bed, because some Devo starts whistling in the dark?" Her deep voice had a masculine edge, a hardness.

Wimple shook his head with a tired smirk. Devo: Corporate catchword for any socially deviate individual, generally from the menial work force. "No, Miss Strom," he said, "I'm not trying to tell you that I want to call the patrol off. I'm just saying that if we go down there now, we could find ourselves in one hell of a shit storm."

Strom returned the detective's smirk. "Is that so?"

"Yes, ma'am."

"Well, in that case, Detective, move your men on down. I can hardly wait."

Long favored by patrolmen throughout the Greater Los Angeles sprawl, the Nissan-Pontiac Marauder was a formidable machine. With a nine-liter, methane-charged power plant, the vehicle was capable of running down virtually anything on the road, and was virtually unstoppable by anything less than an armor-piercing shell. Long and low, it was not, however, built for comfort, and the off-road shocks always wreaked havoc on Wimple's spine.

He rode shotgun beside Miss Strom: shoulders hard against the polymer seats, feet braced on the floorboards, right hand firm on the sissy bar. Earlier, when Strom had given the order to move out, there had been several whispered complaints from the patrolmen. Now, however, as the three-vehicle convoy descended into the black heart of the city, the radios were silent.

"Why don't you tell me about them?" Miss Strom said, easing the Marauder onto the wastes of First Street.

Wimple shrugged, his eyes scanning the tenement windows above. "There's not really much to tell," he replied. "About eighteen months ago, we start getting reports of a little Devo action from the outlying precincts. Vandalism mostly. Petty stuff. Then come July and one of the IRS stations goes up in smoke. After that, we start finding it spray-painted all over the walls: Night Whistlers."

"Any idea who's behind it?"

"Yeah, we've got some ideas."

Strom's thin lips hardened. "So what's been the problem? Why haven't you cleaned them out yet?"

Wimple lifted his gaze to the long blocks of tenements ahead—to the smashed windows and rotting doorways, the grimy, crumbling brickwork and trashed streets. "Well, let's just say that the Whistlers turned out to be a little more organized than we thought." His voice was dull, noncommittal. She gave him a quick look then went back to scanning the street.

They had entered the lower reaches of Ninth Street, and another long canyon of smog-browned tenements. For the most part, the residents here were members of the semiskilled labor force, popularly known as the Menials, officially referred to in ethnological surveys as the Lower Middle Class. Included among their ranks were whole armies of word processors, retail clerks, delivery boys, receptionists, and secretaries. By and large, their lives were measured out in pitiful production bonuses, worthless stock options, and department store clearance sales. They also, of course, spent a lot time pouring over their lottery tickets, even more in front of their television screens, watching Corporate-controlled programming. Still, no matter how blatant the propaganda, it was more entertaining than their dull existences.

The radio came alive with a harsh metallic burst from the last Marauder in the line: "Possible six-twenty on Hill."

Six-twenty meant curfew violation—which invariably meant Devo action.

Strom dropped her left hand from the steering wheel and activated the dispatch button on the dashboard. "Let's show them a response now, gentlemen." Then bringing the Marauder into a tight turn, she activated the spectral-imaging screen and switched the infrared cameras to the scan mode.

Wimple, however, preferred to use his eyes. He initially saw only a half-glimpsed vision among the heaps of uncollected refuse: a thin, brown figure in a drab-green duffle coat. For a moment, a single perverse moment, he actually considered saying nothing. He actually considered returning his gaze to the bleak stretch of road ahead, casually withdrawing another smokeless cigarette and keeping his mouth firmly shut. But even as this thought passed through his mind, the image of the fleeing figure appeared on the screen.

The radio crackled to life again with a voice from the second Marauder. "I've got clean visual."

There was a quick glimpse of a sprinting form beneath a sagging balcony, the sudden clamor of a trash can on the pavement.

Strom powered her vehicle into another hard turn, screeching full-throttle into the adjoining alley. Then, as she deftly lowered her thumb to activate the spotlight, he was suddenly there: a wiry Hispanic huddled beneath an ancient fire escape.

Strom activated the megaphone, and her voice boomed out in harsh, clipped syllables: "Remain where you are! Any attempt to flee will be met with force!"

The figure stumbled back to the alley wall, glaring around like a blinded bull. He was younger than Wimple had first imagined, no more than ten or twelve. His duffle coat was army surplus. His blue jeans were Levi knockoffs. He also wore a pair of black market running shoes—the badge of the Devos.

Strom eased the Marauder to a stop alongside the number two and three vehicles. Then, reaching for the stun gun beneath the dash, she slipped free of her harness and turned to Wimple. "Come on, Detective, let me show you what law and order is all about."

Strom and Wimple approached the suspect slowly. To their left and right, scanning the rooftops with Nikon-Dow Night Vision Systems atop their M-90s, were the four helmeted patrolmen from the backup Marauders. Given the word, they would have been able to pour out some six hundred fragmentation flechettes in less than a fifty-second burst—more than enough to shred the kneeling suspect to a bloody pulp.

Wimple looked at the boy's scared eyes. They kept returning to the stun-gun that dangled from Strom's gloved hand.

Manufactured for Trans Global by Krause-Nova Electronics in Orange County, the XR50 Stun gun had become the last word on hand-held crowd control. It was capable of dispersing a scatter charge of nearly fifty-thousand volts, instantly immobilizing a two-hundred-pound man. At closer range, and against bare skin, the pain was beyond description.

The boy could not keep himself from shivering when Strom laid the cold tip of the stun gun against his cheek, could not keep himself from mouthing a silent plea. In response, however, Strom merely smiled, and turned to Wimple again.

"Why don't you see what he's carrying, Detective? Hmm? See what our little lost lamb has in his pockets."

Wimple pressed the boy facedown to the pavement, consciously avoiding the terrified eyes. He then lowered himself to a knee and mechanically began the search. On the first pass, he withdrew only a greasy deck of playing cards, a half-eaten chocolate bar, and a stainless steel identity tag made out to one Julio Cadiz. Then, almost regretfully, he slowly peeled a six-inch steak knife from the boy's left ankle.

"Well, well, well." Strom smiled. "What have we here?"

Wimple rose to his feet, turning the steak knife over in his fingers. "These things don't necessarily mean much."

Strom let her smile sag into another smirk. "Is that so, Detective?"

"It's just kind of a status symbol with these kids. They don't ever really use them. They just like to carry them around to show off to their buddies."

But by this point, Strom had already withdrawn a pair of keyless handcuffs . . . had already released the safety on the stun-gun.

She secured the boy's wrists behind his back, then yanked up his coat and T-shirt to expose the base of the spine. Although once or twice the boy emitted a pleading whimper, he still hadn't actually spoken.

"Tell your men to secure the area," Strom said as she hunkered down on the pavement beside the handcuffed boy. Then again when Wimple failed to respond: "Secure the area, Detective. Tell your men."

Wimple glanced over his shoulder to the blank faces of the patrolmen. Before he actually gave the order, however, he turned to the woman again. "Look, I'm not trying to tell you how to do your job, Miss Strom, but this is not going to get us anywhere. You understand what I'm saying? And this is not a safe place for us to be wasting our time."

Strom ran a contemplative hand along the gleaming shaft of the stun-gun, then dropped her gaze to the shivering boy. Not looking at Wimple, she finally said, "Detective, I think you should get your men to secure the area before this little brat starts screaming and brings out the whole neighborhood."

She waited until the patrolmen posted on the corner fixed their night vision systems on the balconies and rooftops and chambered clips of flechettes into their weapons. Then very gently, very slowly, she pressed the cold tip of the stun gun to the boy's naked spine.

"Look—" Wimple began.

"Shut up, Detective," she said, her eyes cold, then lowered her gaze back to the boy.

"Well, now, young man. You and I are going to have a little heart to heart. You understand? A frank exchange of views, with you starting first."

An involuntary shudder crossed the thin, feral face of the boy. "Look, lady, I don't know—"

She clamped her hand to his mouth. "No, no, no. That's not how this game is played, my little friend. In this game, you don't speak until I ask a question. Got it?"

The boy may have tried to nod, but Strom had taken hold of his hair. Then, yanking back his head so that his ear was only inches from her lips, she whispered, "Whistlers, my little man. How about telling me what you know about the Whistlers?"

The boy responded with another frenzied shiver, then possibly attempted to mouth some sort of response. But by this time Strom had released his head, activated the stun gun, and pressed the tip home.

The boy seemed to react in definite stages to the voltage, first arching up like a quivering fish, then growing wide-eyed and ridged as the scream tore out of his body. And even when it stopped, he still seemed to have difficulty breathing, while the left leg continued to tremble.

"Now, let's try it again, shall we?" Strom cooed. "Who . . . are . . . the Whistlers?"

The boy shook his head before answering in spluttering gasps. "Look, lady, I don't know what you're talking about. I swear to God. The Whistlers, that's just something that they write on the walls."

"Who writes it on the walls?"

"I don't know. Just some of the Devos around here. I don't know who they are."

"Just some of the Devos, huh? Well, I'm sorry, young man, but that's just not good enough." And lifting up his T-shirt again to expose the base of his spine, she laid down another fifty-thousand volts.

There was something horrifying about the way the boy's eyes grew impossibly wide as he thrashed on the pavement with another trailing scream. There was also something chilling about the way Strom's lips twisted up in a smile as she watched.

Wimple turned his head away, stared for a moment into some distant blackness. Finally, unable to stand the sobs any longer, he approached again.

"Look, don't you think that's enough, Miss Strom? *Miss Strom!*"

She slowly turned on her haunches to face him, her left hand still toying with the boy's sweat-drenched hair. "You got a problem, Detective?"

Wimple met her gaze for a full three seconds before answering, a full three seconds to taste the woman's hatred. "Yeah," he finally nodded. "I got a problem. Quite apart from my personal objection to this activity, I'd like to point out that you are seriously endangering my men. If you think that this neighborhood is asleep right now, you are sadly mistaken. The people up in those buildings know exactly what's going on down here. They know exactly what you're doing, and I can assure you that they don't like it."

She withdrew her fingers from the boy's hair, and his head lolled back to the vomit-smeared pavement. "Well, now, that's very interesting, Detective. Because, you see, I *want* them to know what's going on here. I *want* them to hear every decibel of this little bastard's scream and, remember it—"

"Shut up!"

"How dare you tell me to—"

"Shut up and listen!" Wimple said, as the first cold notes of the solitary whistler wafted down from the blackened rooftops.